Cooper Ridge, The Wonder Kid

Cooper Ridge, The Wonder Kid

Reji Laberje

To order additional copies of this book, contact:
Xlibris Corporation
1-888-795-4274
www.Xlibris.com
Orders@Xlibris.com
48845

Dedication

To my sister, Stacy, who introduced me to the illustration, (from Christ Van Allsburg's "The Mysteries of Harris Burdick"), that served as my inspiration.

Special thanks to the 2006-2007 4th grade class of Tammy Barnes of William A. Diggs Elementary School in Waldorf, Maryland. They were the wonderful first audience for this story.

To my husband, Joe, for his help with the cover photography and his support of this project.

Lastly, to all who support Special Olympics; especially those participants who prove again and again that the human spirit has boundaries far beyond those of the human body.

–and, I could add that "Mat Hill" was of course the inspiration for "Matt Hill". Enjoy! –t.

Chapter 1

The Wonder Kid

Cooper was having the game of his life. By the third inning, he had caught three flies that came his way out there in deep left field. He had assisted on two double plays by the bottom of the fourth; and, in the top of the fifth, he batted in the run that put his team, The Washington Wonderboys, up by one.

Victory hung like a cold glass of lemonade out of reach in the perfect seventy degree air that flowed in gentle breezes, carrying the scent of hot dogs and popcorn, over the little league field. They wanted it. They could see it, feel it, taste it . . . but not reach it . . . not yet.

The sun shone warmly down on the back of the young Wonderboy's neck. Cooper's dad, burnt from the weeks spent watching his son play ball, paced back and forth in front of the silver, metal, bench-style bleachers. They were full to capacity and lined up as deep as a stadium behind the chain link fence that separated the spectators, mostly parents, from the little league pride of western Washington State.

Cooper's best friend, Matt Hill, spun the ball in his chalked up left hand. That lefty had also had a great game. In the past, though, Matt had choked when the win was this close. Cooper tried to send positive thoughts his friend's way across the dust-stirred grass field. The tension was so thick that he could nearly feel the energy bounce right off the diamond back to him. Matt shuffled his feet on the mound, shifting his weight from right to left and back again. It was a sign of frustration Cooper had often noticed when his friend was angry at himself. The other team, on Matt's last pitch to the previous batter, had stolen a base and now the tying run was on third with the win on first. The count was full for this batter; three balls, two strikes. If Matt could get off just one more strike, The Wonderboys would remain champs for one more year of glory. They would be treated as kings rather than the young boys they were.

At last, Matt took a heavy breath, deeply shrugged his shoulders, and lowered his eyes, tightening his focus on the home plate. Cooper sensed how tired his friend felt after playing the full six innings. His empathy for the Wonderboys' pitcher caused the sort of anxiety that came when carrying an overfull glass of purple grape juice across Grandma's new white carpet to the table on the other side of the room. The short trip to victory seemed miles away.

Cooper braced his knees; he was at the ready in a half-squat with his arms loose and anxious. He swallowed hard. His saliva was thin, warm and salty and the gulp only added to the butterflies in his stomach. He knew that Matt's fastball was the best in the league, but Cooper felt like an eternity passed in that moment after the pitch left his friend's hand. He prepared himself to push off into a run as he heard the crack of the bat against the ball echo in his ears.

Time stood still.

He was sure the crowd must be roaring, but in his world, Cooper's only focus was on the ball coming toward him. He imagined hearing the whir of it buzzing through the air. The space around the white sphere became blurry and the ball itself seemed to grow larger as it neared. It was over Matt, past the shortstop and not anywhere near foul or center. It was Cooper's play; no doubt. He couldn't move deep enough—left enough—fast enough toward the now falling baseball. He felt every muscle quiver as he raced to the would-be homer and simultaneously spotted the runner on third making his way to a home-run. That opponent seemed to be moving faster and further toward his goal than Cooper was to his own. In fact, he was sure he was moving in slow motion. As the stitches on that fly came into focus and it began to lose its wings, though, Cooper gained his and—with an amazing push for a boy of only twelve—he was airborne. Cooper stretched his tall body and extended his long arm to its maximum reach. With a resounding SMACK, a beautiful sting ran from his palm down his arm, to his shoulder, across his collar bone, down his spine, through his tense, elongated legs and

calves and straight to his tingling toes that then slammed into the
ground followed by the rest of his slumping body.

He had the ball.

As he clumsily stood up in disbelief, Cooper's world came back
into focus. The cheering and applause of the crowd was deafening.
He wasn't sure if it had just begun or if it had been going all along.
Cooper leapt high in the air—oblivious to any game pains—to loud
background chants of, "WONDER KID! WONDER KID!"

It was a title he had earned and was proud to hear called while
his teammates rushed him.

"WONDER KID! WONDER KID!"

Cooper heard the cry over the cheers and hoots of his fellow
players. Matt and the other boys jumped and screamed when their
coaches joined the huddle.

"WONDER KID! WONDER KID!"

The chant continued.

Finally, squeezing between the broad shoulders of the older
ball players, Cooper spotted his proud father grinning as widely as
a crocodile. Instead of the half hugs that are acceptable for boys,
anything goes after a winning competition. Cooper's dad pulled him
down off a set of shoulders upon which he had been hoisted and he
squeezed him into a full bear hug. He held Cooper back and looked
into the crystal blue eyes that were nestled deep in his tanned face.
As such an athletic boy, Cooper was already the spitting image of
his young dad. Cooper smiled back with his perfect, white-toothed
grin.

"WONDER KID! WONDER KID!"

The calls boomed around the Ridge men.

The elder Ridge pushed Cooper's hat backward off his head and
he ruffled his son's thick, brown mop-top.

"WONDER KID! WONDER KID!"

The Wonderboys team members picked up the cheers as the
sounds of the exiting crowds began to die away. Cooper's dad planted
a flat, hard kiss on his son's forehead.

"Dad!" said a mock angry Cooper. "Not in front of the guys."

"I can't help it, son. I'm so proud! That's my boy they're cheering.
The Wonder Kid! My son, Danny Mills. Danny Mills, The Wonder
Kid," he responded.

Cooper cocked his head in confusion. His father's face began to fade, followed by the little league scene that surrounded him. He turned his head shamefully to one side and—just before feeling that familiar, warm tickle in his ear, he heard the distant, muffled ringing of, "DANNY MILLS, THE WONDER KID! DANNY MILLS, THE WONDER KID . . ."

Chapter 2

Elation to Bitterness

Cooper opened his eyes in a state of disorientation and shook his head back and forth. It was the only part of his body that he could move since a car accident eight years ago. He was paralyzed from the neck down. The same accident killed his father. So, from the time he was four, Cooper was little more than a very wild imagination attached to a very idle body.

He had just had one of his dreams. Tonight, he got to be one of his very favorite characters: *Cooper Ridge, The Wonder Kid.* Cooper dreamed often and his dreams always felt real.

Sometimes, in his dreams, he was a regular student in a regular school with regular friends. Sometimes, he ran and played with the dog that lived down the block and sometimes, on quiet nights, he would simply dream he was taking a walk down a cool, calm street in town . . . just a simple walk . . . simple to anyone who could do it, anyway. To Cooper, those *ordinary* dreams were some of his most peaceful and satisfying.

Tonight, though, he didn't dream about being ordinary. He dreamed he was extraordinary. When Cooper was The Wonder Kid, he was a hero. He swore down to the soles of his feet that he really felt his arms moving; he really felt his legs pounding the ground; he really felt his heart throbbing in his chest. Most of all, during those dreams, he really felt joy.

Then, the dream would end and the nightmare would begin . . . the nightmare that was his life. Somebody in his dream would call him by a different name—by the name Danny Mills. Then, he was snapped back to the reality that he was not Cooper Ridge, The Wonder Kid. In fact, he was not even Cooper Ridge the student or Cooper Ridge who played with the neighborhood dog. He was not even the ordinary boy walking down a cool, calm, street on a quiet night in town. He felt like Cooper Ridge, The Worthless Kid.

So, when he awoke from those hero dreams, (always after a warm tickle in the ear that was not against his pillow), his elation would immediately melt away to bitterness.

Cooper heard a tiny motor and a rushing of air. It was his mattress. It was programmed to fill and release air to and from different chambers within it every fifteen minutes. This made sure that his body didn't get bad sores from constant pressure. The bedsores, or, pressure sores, would need to be drained of blister-like juices or they could lead to serious infections or even the need to amputate body parts.

As the sound of the flowing air ceased, he realized that the tickle in his ear itched and needed to be scratched. Cooper turned his head and pushed the offending ear hard against his pillow. Then, he nodded to scratch much as a bear would rub against a tree trunk to soothe a back itch. Cooper huffed a self pitying sigh as the thought that a bear had more value in life than he did, passed through his mind.

It's not that Cooper was a negative person. He lived a pretty good life. The *sorry-for-himself* attitudes usually only made their voices heard in his own head. He couldn't stop them there.

He arched his neck and rolled back his eyes to read the glowing, green numbers on the clock over his bed. It was 4:30 in the morning. His mother wouldn't be up for another two and a half hours. He put his head back down. There was no point in pretending that he could do more than lay there.

He didn't know whether he was more angry at himself for having the dream or jealous of Danny Mills for being the real Wonder Kid. As he lay there, though, staring at the ceiling, he wished that tonight's dream had only been about Cooper Ridge, an Ordinary Kid.

Chapter 3

The Morning Routine

He may have dozed back to sleep. Cooper wasn't sure. If he did, it was a dreamless sleep and that was a good thing.

At 7:00, Cooper began hearing the familiar sounds of the morning routine. First, there was the annoying beep of his mother's alarm, then her shuffling hand on the nightstand followed by her fumbling slap on the snooze button. It would be seven minutes of quiet before the beginning of the other signs of the start of a new day.

Cooper was good at listening; and at watching. Before he could move his chair on his own and when he would be at a family gathering, he'd often say how unoffended he was to be left in one room when everybody else went to another. Then, alone, all he'd have to do is listen and watch. He rarely called for them. He found it embarrassing; like a baby having to cry from his crib. Eventually, somebody would say something and they'd realize Cooper had been left.

Cooper never got upset about it as long as he got to observe good conversations. He assumed he had a greater appreciation for all of his senses because he didn't have the ability to use his arms and legs. There were days when he'd get taken for a walk in the park and he'd catch himself completely enraptured in another child's moment, listening to and watching him.

Cooper rolled his head and eyes back again to read the clock. He sighed. It was 7:14 when he heard his mother's slippered feet sweeping down the hardwood floors of the hallway. She must have needed an extra snooze. Cooper's mom creaked his door open slowly and tiptoed across the room to his window where she opened the baseball-motif curtains and pulled up the shade to reveal the open window (which was how Cooper liked it to be left while he slept and, living in Arizona, this wasn't a problem for most of the year). The morning light shone in on the walls that were covered with baseball pennants from all of Cooper's favorite World Series winning teams. She looked down at her pride and joy.

"Oh, hey Bud," she whispered with a smile. "You're already awake. I hope it hasn't been long," she added as she sat next to her son on the bed.

"No," he lied. Cooper hated the sound of his voice in the morning before he sat up. He was always hoarse and the words gargled out with an unattractive blend of phlegm. He slept propped up a little bit on pillows, but it wasn't enough. "I heard your alarm is all."

"You look good this morning," his mom's voice was sweet. "I swear the color in your cheeks is wonderful. You sneaking off to play ball games at night or something?" she joked.

Cooper's mind flashed back to one of his hits the night before as Danny Mills in his dream. Of course, his mother was only teasing. She couldn't know about his dreams of The Wonder Kid or any of the other characters whose lives he escaped into while he slept. This was just the sweet, small talk she made each morning to distract him from the embarrassment of being manhandled. His mom was pretty amazing that way.

Before he would even realize what was happening, she had straightened out Cooper's legs and arms and taken off his clothes. She'd change a small bag, called a colostomy bag that was attached to him via tubes. (Cooper couldn't go to the bathroom on his own . . . he couldn't even feel when he had to. The tubes and bags did the job for him and April would change them and clean Cooper as needed.) Then, she'd pull up his sheet again, leave the room, turning on his favorite radio station on the way out and when she returned she would sponge bathe him and simultaneously rub his muscles. She looked Cooper in the eye the whole time and spoke about things that interested him and, the next thing he knew, she was pulling on his daytime clothing.

That was the thing with Cooper's mom. She never made a production of having to coddle and nurse Cooper the way she did. She treated him as *normally* as he imagined other mothers treated their *normal* sons.

"Guess what," she said as she pulled him in a hug toward her and she began to massage Cooper's back, much as one would massage a baby who spends a lot of time in a car seat. It was just one way of preventing bedsores or other raw spots on Cooper. "I've been saving the catalogs for a couple of weeks now, so later in the week we can go through them and pick out new clothes. Then, maybe we can plan a shopping day with Uncle Harry and we'll all go to lunch and get hair cuts."

"Sounds good," Cooper choked out. His voice was already beginning to sound better. His mom massaged his back and his upper chest and throat.

He loved that his mom didn't make him dress in the sorts of clothes he saw on other *special* kids. Special was another word he hated. Special was how he thought those other kids sometimes looked when their parents dressed them in things like too-small striped, buttoned t-shirts and high-water black jeans with beige stitching and—of course—the signature white, leather tennis shoes that didn't look like they belonged to either a boy or a girl, but rather an eighty year old candy striper. Worse still was when parents seemed to think nothing of topping those candy striper shoes off with a pair of black socks with no elasticity left. No. Cooper got to dress like other kids his age and, almost as important, he got to have a decent haircut, too.

He wasn't special when he went out with his mom; he was just another kid—except that he was in a wheelchair. Granted, he didn't exactly look like Danny Mills, The Wonder Kid, either. Cooper's skin—short of his face—was very fair, having rarely seen the sun over the last eight years. His eyes were hazel, like his mom's. His body was soft, as opposed to muscular and, since he was never seen standing, he was hardly ever considered to be tall. His knees were a little on the knobby side and, although he wasn't "all skin and bones", he was hardly thick around the middle, either. His hair didn't have that shine and thickness from sun and sport like Danny Mills', either. He had short, brown hair that was usually cut a little long on top and so short it was practically shaved on the sides and in back. Cooper caught a glimpse of himself in a glass pane of his window and imagined what it would be like to be handsome and athletic like The Wonder Kid.

"I'll grab your chair, Coop," she said. "Do you want to sit up or lay back down?"

"Up, please."

At last, Cooper's voice sounded like a normal twelve-year-old boy. He smiled at his mom. She winked back seeming to know that he was grateful for every effort she made to help him out—even if it was just sitting him up and massaging him or helping to make his voice sound better.

He was propped up against his simple, hospital style headboard with a pillow and his legs were stretched out before him on the bed. She turned off his specialized mattress and left his side to retrieve his chair.

When did his mom pull up the covers beneath his legs? Man, she was good.

His mom returned from across the room with his chair. They had a routine for this, too. Cooper's mom, April, was not a particularly large woman. She was barely over five feet tall and always wore her dark hair in very short, uneven curls. She rarely wore makeup or perfume because she said she had no need for such frills. April had warm, chestnut brown eyes, tiny, high cheekbones, thin, pink lips and a perfect, button nose. Around the house, she was usually in tank tops and shorts with flip flops or slip-on tennis shoes.

April was strong from years of working with her son, though. So, her frail appearance seemed to melt away when you saw her slide Cooper effortlessly into his chair. She would pull the wheelchair up to the bed, and slide Cooper to the edge, then, lifting him at the middle with her shoulder, she would hoist him into his chair. She gently rolled his upper body against the back of the chair and shifted him into the center of the seat. April had to put Cooper's hands in place next, on the arms of the chair. Then, she'd massage and put pressure on the soles of his feet to keep them strong and correctly shaped—just one of many routines to keep his body working properly—and she'd place them onto specially formed foot rests on the chair. She'd pull soft straps over his hands and feet next so that they wouldn't fall. Last, she'd push a small button on his chair that performed similar air-pressure transfers in the cushion and back of the chair as the air tubes in his bed's mattress did. He didn't have it on at all times—just enough to help prevent sores since he spent so much time in the chair.

His wheelchair was very advanced, even beyond the sore-preventing cushions. After April placed her son's head in the pillow rest that kept him from looking like what he called a Cooper Ridge Bobble Head, she pulled a tiny remote control up to his mouth. It was something like a joystick, only very small. When he wore it, he looked like he was wearing one of those microphones that pop singers had on when they did concerts. At first, the independence of moving from a manual chair to a remote control in his own power was overwhelming to Cooper, but he soon grew to love the freedom he had in this newer chair. Cooper was a pro at operating his joystick. He would use his lips, teeth and tongue to move the remote and that was how he controlled his wheelchair. He prided himself on the ability to make turns as quickly and accurately as those he knew who could operate their chairs by hand.

"Do you want to be pushed or do you want to remote?" asked April.

"Pushed for now," said Cooper. His mouth was dry before morning breakfast and it sometimes made working his chair on his own difficult. After they ate was usually when April would brush her son's teeth. Cooper didn't like the way the toothpaste made his foods taste. So, April agreed to hold off the brushings and the grooming time until after her shower and before his schooling.

April pushed her only child down the long hallway, toward the bathroom, past the closet full of his disability supplies.

They affectionately referred to the closet as the hospital gift shop or just the gift shop. Many of the items within it were donated by the doctors, nurses and others who had cared for Cooper in those first two years after the accident during which nobody was sure he'd ever be able to go home at all. There were all sorts of physical therapy items and aids as well as "toys" like dictation machines, audio books and other things to make a disabled life more enjoyable. Also in the closet were oxygen tanks and tubes should Cooper ever need to be hooked up to a ventilator again. Most quadriplegics needed this sort of equipment, but Cooper had a special pacemaker implanted years ago to help his diaphragm keep expanding and contracting to breathe normally.

As they continued down the hall, there was his mother's room in which she had her own bathroom, then a second bathroom complete with a special sit-in shower for Cooper which was a hot tub of sorts with massaging jets. There was also a handicapped toilet. Although, more often than the handicapped toilet, his mother would use the special colostomy bag disposal can in the bathroom. A home service came and picked up the bio-trash every other day. A turn at the end of the hallway to the kitchen came next. Past the eat-in kitchen and pantry was a living room with a television and, then, a home office.

Cooper rarely went down to the basement to which there was a door off of the office. He had to use a special riding chair that was attached to the railing, which was fine, but they never managed a practical means of getting his too-wide wheelchair down the too-narrow, old-fashioned, cellar-style stairs. So, he had to use his manual, folding wheelchair in the basement and Cooper hated having to give up the ability to move on his own. It wasn't a huge loss, though, as the basement contained little more than a washroom and storage.

To the other side of the kitchen was Cooper's study room. It had once been an enclosed porch but was converted for his school needs. He had a table-like desk and there was a projector. His homework tools, many and varied, were kept there so that he could use them almost completely independent of assistance. He was tutored in that room and there was a large open space with mats lain down and exercise machines on which he would receive daily physical therapy.

When they got to the kitchen, Cooper's mom parked him at the low counter and proceeded to make her coffee.

"You feeling up to solids today?" April questioned her son.

"No," he said. Cooper's solid foods were really not solid the way most people have; steaks were never on the menu. (Although, he did get to suck a piece of a steak once and he remembered loving it. It was at a very fancy restaurant where the meat was tender enough for him to enjoy.) Some days, though, he was able to manage scrambled eggs and cooked vegetables or—when he was really lucky—banana cream pies . . . mmm . . . Cooper loved bananas. A solid breakfast was usually very thin oatmeal or cream of wheat.

When Cooper ate various solids, he needed a lot of help and he had to eat very slowly. He nearly choked one time and was lucky that his Uncle Harry had been there. He punched Cooper in the stomach. It sounds crazy, but that was actually easier than wrestling Cooper out of the wheelchair and attempting the Heimlich maneuver on his limp body. Immediately Cooper shot the food out of his mouth. He yelled at his uncle, (more out of embarrassment and frustration than actual anger), and then the two of them laughed about the incident as soon as later that same day. It had since become a family joke. Cooper's Uncle Harry would walk into the kitchen punching one fist into his other palm and ask, "So, what's for dinner, tonight, Guy? Rocketing Ragu? Projectile pea soup? Shooting shellfish?"

Most of Cooper's meals could be taken through a straw. His mom tried very hard to keep them exciting and varied so that Cooper didn't get bored. She did make sure the meals were healthy, though—just to ensure that his digestion wouldn't be difficult. This morning he had blended yogurt and banana. His mom threw in a couple of crushed graham crackers, too. She stayed in the room while he drank his breakfast in case there was a problem. Then, she turned on a small television screen on the counter so that Cooper could watch his favorite morning show while she left the room to shower and dress for the day.

Chapter 4

School

Just like other kids his age, Cooper did have to have classes. Year-round, in fact! He thought it was a bum deal, really. He had all the work but none of the socializing. Instead, he had a private tutor that came to his home during the day. He had reading, writing and arithmetic; he had science, social studies and specials. Of course, his music and art was more about identifying and appreciating than it was about applying. He did try to sing sometimes, but not being able to feel his own lungs and diaphragm made it difficult at best to breathe right. So, Cooper was pretty sure he'd never be presenting any operas. Several times, he tried some painting while holding the brush in his teeth. He managed to perfect making several rather crooked shapes and he could legibly write his own name, but nothing more advanced than that. Twice a month, he got to go to the pool with his Uncle Harry for mobility exercises. Cooper also had to learn about sports—even though he never dared to have the hope to play them. Several times a day, April would come in and clean him up and help him if he had any bathroom necessities.

His classes and homework were done with a combination of special reading machines, a computer that printed the words he spoke and audio books. He even had CDs and DVDs included for helping him to learn. As far as disabled kids went, Cooper was downright spoiled.

All of his classes were taught by a private tutor named Derek Lowell. Mr. Lowell was very strict. He would arrive precisely on time each day and he kept the same tight schedule expected for kids in a regular, public school. He specialized in "special needs" children. (There was that word that Cooper hated.) So, Cooper had expected the worst when his mom hired him when he began second grade. For Kindergarten and first grade, April had home schooled Cooper; then, she had to get a job to make ends meet.

Mr. Lowell surprised him, though, by not treating him *special* at all. As a matter of fact, Mr. Lowell was relatively hard on Cooper. He expected him to know the same things as the *normal* kids. Mr. Lowell expected him to pretend that he was really learning for real life—as if he would ever get a chance to grow up and be an adult on his own.

Once, he even brought Cooper to a baseball game and made him keep stats on his dictation machine. He felt ridiculous saying numbers aloud to himself throughout the game, but was rewarded afterward with a visit to the locker room. One of the players presented Cooper with a bat and said it was his to use when he got better one day. The news crews ate that up. *Got better!* That's one of those stupid things people say when they think they're being thoughtful and encouraging to handicapped children before they even realize the child's condition. (Cooper insisted the gesture didn't help at all but he did keep that bat in his room, right against his window ledge.)

As for Cooper getting tiptoed around in the rest of his studies . . . well, there was no special attention on account of his special needs. If Cooper had shortcomings, Mr. Lowell would say, they all fell below the neck. And he, as Cooper's teacher, was only concerned with what went on above the neck. The rest was the job of his physical therapist. In short, from the neck up—he promised his mom—Cooper would be a 4.0.

In other words, Cooper loved Mr. Lowell.

So, for the past two years, did his mom. He hoped that one day Mr. Lowell would ask to marry her. He even looked to Cooper a lot like Danny Mills' father from his dreams. If Cooper could only do it, he would dance for the people in his life. He knew that he was lucky to have such a wonderful extended family.

Dancing was a dream, but important to a boy in his situation, was physical education. Yes, even Cooper had PE. Each day ended the same way; with his mom's sister (his Aunt) May coming to help him with his physical therapy. Cooper always thought his aunt and mom had funny names. His mom, who was born in May, had the name April and his aunt, who was born in April, had the name May.

Cooper's Aunt and mother couldn't look more different! Where April was tiny and petite, May was tall and round. Where April wore trendy clothes and hairstyles, May was almost always in sweats with her long, straight hair swept back in a bun or low ponytail. But, Aunt May did have a big, beautiful smile and when she entered a room, Cooper couldn't help but feel warmed by her presence.

Aunt May was a nurse and she was a blessing for Cooper and his mother. Without her, they probably couldn't afford the sort of personal care he needed every day. Plus, she was married to Cooper's Uncle Harry who was a really great guy. He did construction work and he always made sure all of his buildings were handicap-accessible so that Cooper could visit him at his sites. Also, as a big, strong man, he always came along on day trips in case Cooper or his chair needed to be carried anywhere in which his Uncle had no say in the building plans.

"Hey, Coop," his Aunt May said when she came by later. "You ready for a hardcore workout, today? We'll get those arm and leg muscles in check."

"I don't really see the point, Aunt May," he grumbled. "I was planning on holding off on that miraculous recovery," Cooper attempted as a joke to cover up his accidental negative comment. Aunt May was most insistent that he stay positive.

"Well, we've talked about this more times than I can count, hon," she began, as she took his blood pressure, temperature and resting pulse. "In your case, it's not about trying to regain movement. It's about trying to keep your muscles strong enough to protect your body and about keeping your circulation healthy. Besides, I don't deal with that whining attitude, do I?"

"Yeah, yeah," Cooper sighed as his aunt stretched and bent, twisted and massaged his arms and his legs. She turned his feet and hands at the joints and ran his legs by bending his knees like a bicycle. She'd push the soles of his feet against different blocks of wood, rubber foam and other materials—keeping them strong and properly shaped. Half of the time, Cooper stayed in his chair and half of the time was spent on the floor mats. Plus, he got a massage every day while lying on his stomach on a special padded table. Aunt May was good at what she did, but she wasn't as good at hiding the fact that she was doing it as his mom was. As grateful as he should have been, he always felt ridiculous during his physical therapy.

His aunt took his heart rate again, and then put down her hand with the wristwatch in frustration. "That's strange. Okay, before I take all of your vitals again, I'm going to put you on the autos."

"But, it's Monday!" complained Cooper.

The autos were the nickname Aunt May gave to refer to any of the machines to which she would attach Cooper. He sat in them while the machine would lift his arms and his legs on its own. Cooper felt more like a robot than a boy on the autos; prisoner to the commands his aunt had pre-entered. He tolerated the exercise in circulation and humiliation because he usually only had to do them on Tuesdays and Thursdays plus some mornings on the weekends with his mom.

"I know, but usually, Oh-So-Strong-Nephew-Of-Mine, your heart rate rises from the physical therapy. Today it hasn't. So, I want to exercise you a little bit more before I check your stats again." She spoke to Cooper as she hooked his arms and legs onto the rubber foam paddles that would lift his various appendages.

"Fine," he huffed, as though he were giving her permission to do what she had already done.

"I'm glad you approve, *Doctor* Cooper!" she joked. "I've set it for 15 minutes. I'm going to talk to your mom for a bit. Okay?"

"All right," he resigned.

Chapter 5

A Growing Boy

Except for the times that April helped to clean up Cooper or change his colostomy bags, (which were kept discreetly in a black Velcro pouch at the back of his wheelchair while the tubes were concealed in black elastic wraps and beneath his attire), she made herself scarce during the day so that Mr. Lowell and her sister could do their work. She ran a small online business from home, reselling items found at garage sales and thrift stores she'd visit with Cooper, and she had very little to accomplish away from the home office. This way, she was always there if she was needed, but was not around to be a disturbance for Cooper if she didn't have to be.

When Aunt May arrived for physical therapy, Mr. Lowell would visit with April in her office for a little bit before leaving. His aunt hated to intrude. Cooper listened very hard over the buzzing of the autos to hear what she had to say to his mom.

"Hey Derek, how are you?" she asked Mr. Lowell.

"Good. Good, May, and you?" he returned.

"Fine. I don't mean to interrupt," she began.

"Oh, hush with the formalities, May! You're family!" scoffed Cooper's mom. "What's going on?"

"Well, it's nothing, I'm sure. But . . . well . . . it's Cooper," she said at a loss for words.

"What do you mean?" asked April sounding immediately concerned.

"It's not bad, April. Let me sit," she added, still not looking sure of herself or her reason for the conversation that she had begun. She fidgeted in the chair and stared back and forth between the door, into which the sounds of the autos were quietly whispering, and April. Finally, she sighed audibly and looked at her sister.

"Have you been doing the regular routines with him, lately? Same exercises? Nothing strenuous?"

"Sure. I mean, yes. I can't think what you mean. But, nothing has changed around here. I'm certainly not pushing him," said April, almost defensively.

"No, it's not that."

"Is—he—okay?" April asked deliberately.

"Yes. I told you! Well, I've noticed for a little while, now."

"Noticed what?"

"I'm getting there, sis, relax! Cooper's muscles are becoming . . . this is just strange . . . well, they're becoming developed," Aunt May finished.

"That's good, isn't it," questioned Mr. Lowell?

"It's great," she exclaimed. "It just doesn't make sense is all."

"You're just doing a great job is all. I knew you were the best," said April glowingly.

"I wish I could take the credit," May huffed proudly, "but it's not me. It's not just that he's a growing boy, either . . . almost a teenager already, if we can believe that. It's not just Cooper's muscles; it's his heart rate, too. His resting pulse is fabulous and, today, I couldn't even get him up to his target heart rate. I know this sounds ridiculous, but Cooper's cardiovascular system is like that of an athlete and, April, it is a good thing. I just don't understand it. I mean, we've talked about this to a certain extent in the past. Most people who are as severely paralyzed as Cooper, especially from an accident as opposed to from birth, have a certain limit on life."

"Oh, May—" cut in Mr. Lowell.

"Don't stop me. You know what I say is true, Derek. So do you, April. Now, I'm not just talking about the value of life; I think we all do well to keep him happy. *You* do well, April. I know it's hard for you to hear, but I'm talking about the length of life. The body doesn't stay healthy when it is forced to be idle for so long. The body is not made to be still. The muscles begin to break down. The heart grows weak from lack of exerting its strength. The lungs even grow weak from the lack of necessity of them to fill to capacity. If I knew of Cooper's situation and didn't know the actual boy, I would say . . .

I'm sorry, but, I would say he is lucky to still be alive. He's beaten the odds and now those odds of him making it even longer are against him," May sighed.

"But, you just said . . ." began Cooper's mother.

"That he's doing great. He is. That *is* what I'm saying. I've been a nurse for sixteen years. I've worked in therapy for twelve of those years, eight of them with Cooper. I've never seen something like this. Your son, my nephew, is as healthy as any twelve-year-old I know. *More* healthy than some of them! I just wish I knew why. There is no logical explanation for his strength and endurance or for the athletic condition of his heart."

"Oh," said April, unsure of how she should respond. "Sorry?"

"I'm not! Just looking for answers and I thought you might know something is all. I thought you may have an idea. I don't know why Cooper is so unusual. I wish I did. The entire medical community would wish to know his magical formula. He's getting better, April. I'm not saying he could move or he could ever even . . . I don't know . . . *dream* of it. His nerves are still dead. They're not making connections. But, his body thinks that it has done so; it thinks it has moved. It's strong," May shrugged. "Well, if we never find the answer, I suppose I'm just selfishly happy that it is happening with my nephew of all people."

The autos let out a beeping sound and slowed to a stop.

"That's the autos, April. Let me see if your son actually has a target heart rate, yet. Thanks for listening," added Aunt May before she made her way back across the house to Cooper the Robot. She took his vitals one last time and his physical therapy was officially over. His mother cleaned him up and he went to do his homework while his mom prepared dinner for him, her and Mr. Lowell who occasionally joined them.

Chapter 6

Mr. Lowell's Loss For Words

After dinner, Cooper got to watch a television show while his mom and Mr. Lowell washed dishes. A short while into the show, Mr. Lowell came in to join Cooper in the living room.

"How's about we sit out on the porch, Cooper?" he asked. "It's a beautiful night."

"Sure," said Cooper. He wasn't really feeling up to remoting just then, but Mr. Lowell did not come to his aid, so he wasn't about to be pushed. *(That was just another of Mr. Lowell's ways of treating Cooper like everybody else.)* He remoted to the specially mounted number pad on the wall where he punched in a door code with his nose and the front door swung open.

The air that night was warm and thick with the scent of the desert shrubbery and red clay stones they had in place of a lawn. Cooper did love the way the evening air settled around him at that perfect time just before the fireflies began to make their lighted nightly appearances, complete with a choreographed, candlelit performance. He could close his eyes and feel the tingle of warmth blend with the occasional cool brushing of a breeze about his face and imagine what it would be like to experience that sensation through to the very tips of his fingers and toes—his every nerve alive and dancing with the splendor of an end of summer, dusk time atmosphere. Cooper took a deep breath and smiled.

"You look well, tonight, Coop," Mr. Lowell said.

"I am," he returned, as he turned his smile upon his teacher and friend who had plopped into the front porch swing, fidgeting slightly.

Mr. Lowell parted his lips as if about to add something more but closed them again before actually speaking.

"What is it?" Cooper questioned.

"We've known each other a long time, haven't we?" Cooper wasn't used to Mr. Lowell, his rather strict tutor, taking this timid route in a conversation. What was he getting at?

"Well, yeah," Cooper said.

"Yes," Mr. Lowell corrected. Some of his teaching qualities still shone through.

"Yes," said Cooper begrudgingly.

"I don't have any kids of my own, of course you already know this, and I don't have a wife, well of course you know that. I mean, I . . . I've been . . . well, you're mom and I we date or . . . you know . . . not date exactly. We hang out I mean. I mean . . . what I mean is . . ."

"I know what you mean," Cooper rescued his teacher from what he himself surely would normally have corrected as a complete run-on, grammatically messed up statement.

"Of course you know," said Mr. Lowell. Then, he just stared blankly at Cooper for a moment with his mouth hanging open void of verbalization before shaking his head and seeming to snap into a restart mode. "Do you want to walk a bit? I'll push," he added quickly when he saw Cooper swallow hard at the question. He could tell that the boy did not want to remote and although this didn't usually stop him from asking as much as possible from Cooper, he seemed to be in an inexplicably tender mood tonight.

"Sure," he answered curiously.

Mr. Lowell got up from the porch swing as abruptly as he had sat down and then he began to push Cooper off the porch down the twisting wheelchair ramp that led first to the driveway and then to the sidewalk beyond.

"It's a beautiful night," he began again the same way he had before they came outdoors.

"Yes, it is," Cooper said, still intrigued by the strange behavior of the teacher.

"The thing is, Cooper," proceeded Mr. Lowell as he pushed the young boy down the walk of the neighborhood, "I really like your mom. You know that. And if you don't know how much I care about you by now, well—" he stopped. "Well, then I'm doing something wrong."

"I do know," Cooper assured him. This was about as heartfelt as words from Mr. Lowell could get and so he realized that this was kind of the equivalent of a father-son moment seeing as Mr. Lowell and his Uncle Harry were the two men that together sort of filled that role for him.

"I think," his teacher continued, "that maybe three people who are around each other as much as we all are . . . well, they're kind of a family, aren't they?"

"I think so," Cooper said. He smiled again now to hear Mr. Lowell sounding as nervous as he'd been known to make Cooper on many tests in the past.

"Well, um, how would you like it, then, if I *were* around more? What I mean to say is—well, if your mom wants me to be and says yes, that is—"

"Yes?" Cooper interjected, suddenly excited. "Mr. Lowell, are you gonna ask mom to get married?"

"I wanted to make sure you were okay with it, first," he said. Mr. Lowell came to a stop on the sidewalk in front of the home of a neighbor and he looked down at Cooper.

"I am," Cooper said as he nodded his head as vigorously as he could. He wanted to say more, but he knew that his teacher understood how cheerful he was. Mr. Lowell put a hand on both sides of Cooper's face. It wasn't a hug, but it meant even more because he knew that Cooper could feel it. The two young men glowed happily. He may have been about to hug Cooper for real, but just then, Hank Rutherford came out to his front yard with his son Nicholas, and their dog, Beaches—named for his sand-colored fur.

Chapter 7

The Neighbor's Memory

"**H**ey, Derek!" called Mr. Rutherford. "Great night, huh?"
"Hank! Yes—it—is!" exclaimed Mr. Lowell in a deliberate announcement as though he were feeling this had just been confirmed. He seemed down right giddy and Cooper thought it was kind of cute and funny the way that this normally tough man would melt when it came to the way he felt for Cooper's mom.

"What are you two gentlemen up to this fine evening?" Mr. Lowell threw gleefully.

"Oh, Nicky has some new trick he's doing with Beaches he wanted to show off to me. Come on up, you two. We'll come down off the porch for Cooper."

Nicholas and Beaches bounded down their wooden porch steps with Mr. Rutherford behind while Mr. Lowell pushed Cooper up their front walk.

"Hey, Coop!" said Nicholas.

"How you doin' son?" said Mr. Rutherford. He patted Cooper on the head the same way he'd pat Beaches. "Nice to get out in the fresh air, isn't it?" Cooper took a deep, calming breath and before he could say anything in return, Mr. Lowell cut in.

"So, what's this new trick of your son's?" He could tell that Cooper was uncomfortable. It wasn't that Mr. Rutherford was mean to Cooper. He just didn't seem to understand that he was twelve-years-old! That was two years older than his own son and he had heard him speak to Nicholas sometimes as though he was grown completely.

Nicholas, on the other hand, who had known Cooper his whole life and been over to play computer games many times through the years, was just the opposite. With what is perhaps the blessing of childhood innocence, he did not know that he should treat Cooper any differently than anyone else. "I'll show you guys. But, Coop, hey! I got a new video game and it's a joystick one and you can use the joystick that has the button in the middle of the top—it's just a one-button game! Maybe you could come by and play this week?"

"Cool," Cooper smiled back. Why was it so simple for Nicholas to talk to him and understand him? He'd add him to the list of people in his extended family that made Cooper so lucky.

"Well, we'll see if that's something he can handle," Mr. Rutherford added with yet *another* pat on the head to Cooper. "Why don't you show us all your trick, Nicky, m'boy?"

"Oh yeah," he remembered. "Coop, watch this! It is *so* cool!"

While Derek and Hank continued in conversation, Nicholas pulled out his prize yo-yo and began to get it started up and down the string. As he rolled the yo-yo down, Beaches laid flat on the ground. When the yo-yo came up, Beaches would stand. Up and down, up and down went the yo-yo and Beaches, too.

"Isn't that awesome?" Nicholas said excitedly. "Here, you do it!"

Nicholas loved playing at yo-yo tricks. He could do walk the dog and around the world and all sorts of other neat things. The year before—with a great deal of patience for a boy of only nine at the time—he had taught Cooper how to do the simple up and down boomerang with the yo-yo. He'd put the string in Cooper's mouth after he had wound it tightly. Then, Cooper could make it go up and down several times if he jerked his head back at just the right time. Nicholas even gave Cooper one of his own, very nice, trick yo-yos. Cooper had made it come back eight times in a row by the end of the summer and he probably could have done even more, but on that eighth snap up, the yo-yo hit Cooper a little too hard in the face and the string popped out of his mouth. The yo-yo fell to the ground and something came loose that meant it was never able to be as tightly wound again. Cooper promised Nicholas he'd have his mom tighten it up and keep practicing, but he'd only gotten to it a couple of times before—like the bat from the professional baseball player—the yo-yo found a resting place in Cooper's bedroom. It was on the nightstand next to his bed, just beneath the light of his bedside lamp.

Cooper really wasn't up to being the trick for Mr. Rutherford, along with Beaches, but Nicholas had already run up to him, pulled down his head and remote pieces on his wheelchair and practically shoved the yo-yo string into Cooper's mouth.

"Oh!" said Cooper in surprise.

"You ready for me to let go?" asked Nicholas.

"Uh-huh," Cooper responded through teeth gritted down onto the string.

Nicholas dropped the yo-yo as it fell from the pulley of Cooper's mouth. Beaches laid down. When Cooper felt the tug of the string, he jerked his head back to recall the yo-yo. It only returned halfway. Beaches stood. The yo-yo then made another descent and Beaches laid down again. This time, Cooper jerked his head back too late and the yo-yo only rose about an inch before simply spinning around at the bottom like a carnival swing. Beaches cocked his long-nosed puppy face to one side, then rolled over onto his back and twisted around on the walkway playfully.

"That's okay, boy," said Mr. Rutherford. Cooper wasn't sure whether he meant him or the dog. He was a little embarrassed. Nicholas, however, was thrilled.

"Cool! You made him roll over! I wanna try!" he exclaimed. He grabbed the yo-yo from Cooper and ran with his dog to a softer place, in the dirt of the front yard.

The men continued in their conversation about things that didn't much interest Cooper; the new construction of nearby homes, some old tool store that closed in town, and bits and pieces about politics and all of those other dull adult subjects. Instead of pretending to be interested in their talk, he focused in on his listening while he intently watched Nicholas and Beaches practicing tricks with yo-yo commands.

Beaches would go up and down to the rhythm of Nicholas' yo-yo and Nicholas would praise him heavily like a parent of a child taking his first steps.

"Now, try this," Nicholas began. He made the yo-yo spin at the bottom of the string. Beaches laid down. "No, Beaches," said Nicholas. Beaches stood back up. "No," said Nicholas.

They practiced going up and down some more, and this time, when Nicholas got to the spinning yo-yo, he dropped it entirely and got on his own back on the ground like Beaches had earlier, rolling over and over. Beaches didn't roll over, though, to mimic his owner. Instead, he playfully pounced on Nicholas.

"Beaches!" Nicholas laughed.

The two rolled around in the yard while Nicholas chuckled and covered his face to protect it from Beaches' licking and gentle pawing. They continued to wrestle about and Cooper couldn't help but grin, too.

"Good boy, Beaches! Good boy!" Nicholas praised. Then, from between the two of them, Cooper saw two fireflies appear seemingly out of nowhere. They were the brightest fireflies he had ever seen, and big, too—more like violet glowing stars—rising up to the sky. He closed his eyes. They'd have to go in, soon, and he wanted to enjoy this moment. When Cooper reopened his eyes, he couldn't see the first fireflies, but throughout the night air, he began to notice the small flickering tails of the winged beacons of night appearing all around him.

"I guess we'd better call it a night, Derek," said Mr. Rutherford.

"Yes, yes, Hank," he said. "We'd better get walking back, too. Goodnight, Nicholas. Great job with Beaches."

"Thanks, Mr. Lowell. See ya, Coop."

"Bye," said Cooper. He continued to listen as he was pushed away and the Rutherfords went indoors.

"Some trick, Nicky. Some trick. I think you've earned some ice cream before bed."

*   *   *

It was just a short while later that Cooper found himself tucked into his bed sheets for the night after his bedtime exercises were completed. His sleeping position was slightly varied from the night before as just one more precaution against bedsores. His curtains were wide open with the window cracked to the sweet, still, desert air. Knowing that, just down the hall, Mr. Lowell would soon be asking his mom to be his wife; Cooper smiled happily and closed his eyes.

The night began noiseless as he slept but eventually he heard the desert crickets begin their evening chirps. At some point, however, Cooper was sure he heard, in place of the crickets' song, tiny voices floating above him in his *then* dreamless sleep. He turned his head dozily to one side and felt a small tickle in the ear that was not against his pillow.

Cooper was running down a set of wooden porch steps. Then he was seeing himself and Mr. Lowell and Mr. Rutherford. He played with a yo-yo and with Beaches. Cooper gave the yo-yo to the boy in his dream that looked like himself. Beaches went up and down and rolled around to the rhythm of the boy's mouth yo-yo.

"Cool! You made him roll over! I wanna try!" Cooper heard his dream self say. He ran with Beaches to the front yard and he trained the yo-yo again and again for the obedient dog. Then, Cooper tried to make Beaches do the same as the boy in the wheelchair had made him do. "No, Beaches," he said to his dog as Beaches laid down. "No," Cooper said as Beaches got back up.

Cooper and his dog practiced some more. Then, Cooper dropped the yo-yo playfully and rolled around on the ground. Beaches joined him and licked him and pawed gently at his covered body. Cooper laughed heartily so that he felt his chuckle shake his body from deep in his gut. He felt Beaches' paw against his shoulder. He felt the wetness of the dog's tongue against his skin. Cooper felt the softness of Beaches' fur. He was happy and living in the moment of playing with *his* dog.

It was time to go in. He ran back up the steps with his dad and with his dog. Cooper smiled joyously.

His dad patted him lovingly on the shoulder as they went into the house. "Some trick, Nicky. Some trick. I think you've earned some ice cream before bed."

Cooper's world grew dim. He lowered his head in confusion at the sound of the name. He felt the tingle of warmth blend with the cool brushing of an end of summer, dusk time breeze. He experienced an energizing sensation through to the very tips of his fingers and toes—his every nerve alive and dancing with the splendor of the atmosphere. He looked past his porch and saw, in the distance, Mr. Lowell pushing away a boy in a wheelchair. Then, there was a warm tickle in his ear.

*   *   *

Cooper opened his eyes in a cloud. It was just a dream. He looked at his open window, letting in the warm air that was still thick with the scents of desert shrubbery and red clay. The crickets were still chirping away in their evening glee.

Cooper heard, from down the hall, a joyful cry of, "Yes!" from his mother in the kitchen. He sighed happily despite the fact that he was now scratching away the itch in his ear, and with it—the too real imaginings of the night, using his nodding against the pillow method. He closed his eyes once again and returned to a peaceful, dreamless sleep.

Chapter 8

A New Kind of Family for Christmas

The next few months were a whirlwind for Cooper. He didn't have time to think about the dreams or visit Beaches and Nicholas as often as usual or any of the other things that usually kept him busy during the hours and days in which he wasn't schooling or doing physical therapy. Mr. Lowell and his mom had decided on a December wedding and preparations were underway to make it a very special ceremony.

Aunt May came by for longer hours these days. Cooper wasn't sure why. She would do his regular physical therapy—complete with the autos every single day. Cooper didn't talk to her about his dreams; he couldn't tell anybody. But, secretly, he wondered if they had something to do with why she had to always put him on the autos these days to get his heart rate up. He knew how hard and heavily his heart throbbed when he slept and dreamt. He knew he felt tired in his muscles until he woke and, only then, did he not feel his heart or muscles at all. Surely if he shared such things, Aunt May wouldn't think him only crippled, she would think him crazy.

After his regular physical therapy, and sometimes during it, Mr. Lowell would now be sticking around or hanging out and Aunt May would be explaining things. Sometimes she was even letting him help. It was strange to Cooper. He loved Mr. Lowell, but this new role of his—one that was so close to his physical handicaps—was an adjustment.

Mr. Lowell also came by earlier in the mornings and stayed later at night, working on plans with his bride-to-be. Cooper's mom was still the one in charge of all of the other morning and end-of-night routines; the ones that involved washing up and dressing or undressing, but Mr. Lowell was sometimes even there when Cooper was still in bed. It all led up to the newest, oddest change of all and that was that he was supposed to call Mr. Lowell, *Derek*. After several years of Mr. Lowell, this was hard and Cooper always found himself having to correct his words.

Although all of the changes and the unusually hectic lifestyle that had settled upon the Ridge, soon-to-be Lowell, household, were hard—Cooper was quietly enjoying every minute. It had been difficult enough throughout his life to not be like other kids physically. When he also had to deal with the fact that his family wasn't like other families, he used to be jealous of simple things like watching a mom and dad have coffee together or sharing a car or talking about who was in charge of what chore or errand. So, Cooper made the changes with a grumble in his voice, but a grin in his heart as he held a secret hope for the future family of which he would get to be a part. His mom was still his mom, Mr. Lowell . . . err . . . *Derek* . . . would be his step-dad and he had a wonderful Aunt and Uncle.

On a couple of occasions, when his mom and Derek were out to choose flowers or food or some other thing for the wedding, Nicholas would have Cooper over to show him the latest video game that Cooper was capable of playing or he'd *force* him to practice his yo-yo. He was actually getting quite good at it! Cooper made the yo-yo return *twelve* times, now!

In short, life was good. The four months since Derek had first proposed until the night before the actual wedding flew by in a happy flurry of familial interactions in which Cooper joyously basked.

Mr. Lowell didn't stay for dinner the night before the wedding. He left right after Cooper's Friday school studies. Aunt May and Uncle Harry joined his mother and him for the meal, instead.

"So, tomorrow's the day, Coop," said Uncle Harry. "You excited?"

"Sure," Cooper replied. "Not as much as Mom, though!"

"You know," began his mom. "A lot is going to change around here, Bud."

"I know. Mr. Lowell . . . I mean, Derek . . . is going to live here now."

"Well, that's not the only thing," said Aunt May. "There's something else we need to tell you, too, Coop."

"What?" he asked.

"Well," she continued, "you know how Mr. Lowell has been learning about your exercises?"

"Yes."

"He's going to be sort of taking over on those and doing your physical therapy with you as well as your school."

"Why can't you and what about Uncle Harry for my days at the pool?"

"I talked to Derek about the pool, too, Cooper," said his uncle. "He'll be working with somebody from the hospital to start with, but he's ready to take over on that, too. I think he'll do okay."

"And I know how to take care of everything, too, honey," his mom added sweetly.

"But why can't you guys?" he repeated.

"I got a new job, Coop," said Aunt May. "It starts at the beginning of the new year, in just a few weeks. We'll be here for the wedding and for Christmas."

"Well, and after, too, right?" Cooper questioned. "Just because you don't work here doesn't mean you can't visit, right?"

"We'll visit," said Uncle Harry, "when we can. The thing is, buddy, your aunt's job isn't nearby."

"Upstate?" he asked.

"*States*, actually," said Aunt May.

"Cooper, honey," said his mom with the air of somebody about to tell a kid that his dog ran away, "Aunt May and Uncle Harry will be moving to Washington State."

"It's a great job. We just couldn't turn it down. Physical therapy with a community recreation department," described Uncle Harry quickly before his nephew could respond.

"For whole teams of young players, Cooper. The community supports two departments, both a Special Olympics side and fully capable athletes. And there's a state facility for disabled children—paralyzed children. I'll be volunteering there once a week, too. Plus, the town even has this championship little league team there. You'd love to watch them play!" Aunt May explained excitedly, continuing where her husband left off.

"And you can, too!" exclaimed Uncle Harry.

"Of course!" his aunt went on. "You're more than welcome to visit maybe as soon as spring when we've gotten settled."

"That should give me plenty of time to fix up the house for you. It's a ranch; all one level. I have to put up a ramp for the front porch, though," said Uncle Harry. "And there's snow on the ground up there right now, so I can't get to working on that right away. But, soon. I promise."

"Oh," he said. "Oh." Cooper didn't know really what else to add. His aunt and uncle had been a part of his daily life and routine for as long as he could remember and it was hard to imagine not having them around. This was a lot to absorb in one sitting.

"We were going to wait to tell you until after the wedding, but then we realized that there may be others there who knew and we didn't want you to find out by accident from one of them instead of from us," said Cooper's mom.

"We should have thought of it sooner," added Aunt May. "We really didn't mean to leave this to the night before the wedding—"

"Sorry about that, Coop," finished Uncle Harry.

"No," he said, "No, it's okay." Cooper added resolutely. He made a choice to go with his Aunt's requisite positive attitude and he realized that it really was okay, after all. Tomorrow his family was changing in a lot of ways but he decided there were more good ways than bad. The truth was that he always knew there could come a day when his mix-and-match family would normalize to the rest of society around them and he couldn't think of a better way to do that than with his mom and his soon-to-be step-dad under one roof. He knew he'd still have Aunt May and Uncle Harry when he needed them. They were family.

They all finished the rest of the dinner in anxious conversations about the next day's events. Then, Uncle Harry and Aunt May helped clean up the dishes and they grabbed their jackets in order to leave.

"See you tomorrow, sis," Aunt May said to Cooper's mom.

"You'll look beautiful, April," added Uncle Harry with a kiss to her cheek.

"Hey, Harry, before you go could you put Cooper on the swing for me?" April asked her brother-in-law.

"You'll be okay to get him back in, afterward?" he asked.

"No problem. I'd just rather you carried him right now since you're here is all," she shrugged.

"Okay, Bud, you're going for a ride," said Cooper's Uncle. He took down the head pieces and unstrapped his nephew from the chair before hoisting up his limp body to be carried to the porch.

Cooper's mom had set a special pillow chair on one side of the front porch swing so that he could sit by her and have his head balanced. April sat on the other side of the swing and waited for her son. Uncle Harry was such a large man, that it was a somewhat contrary act to see how gingerly he would set Cooper at the side of his mother. Then, the gruff uncle that Cooper had come to know and love came out again as he ruffled his nephew's hair ruggedly before setting on his way with Aunt May for the night.

"We love ya, guy!" he muttered.

"Goodnight!" Aunt May called from the car.

Cooper nodded and April waved lightly as they watched them drive off. It was already dark and the night air was slightly chilly. April pulled a light blanket over her son and herself. The fireflies were flickering about in front of them and seeming to float upward into the sea of lights above.

"Gosh, look at that sky," said Cooper's mom dreamily. "A million stars visible tonight."

"Yeah," Cooper agreed as he turned his head to take in the nightscape above them.

"I like when we get to sit out here," began Cooper's mom, "You know that, don't you?"

"'Course, mom."

"Well, I just wanted you to know is all. Not everything has to change. We can still have time for just us. Just like this. We've been through a lot, Bud, you and I."

"Yeah."

"You know, Derek really loves you, too."

"I know," he mumbled embarrassingly.

"Don't say it like that! There's nothing wrong with it, Cooper!"

"I know. It's just that he's not my dad but now he'll be like it, I guess. I mean, kind of. But, I'm happy about it Mom. I really am."

"I do miss your dad, Cooper. But, I know he'd be smiling to see that we have somebody special to help take care of us and love us. You should know that, too."

"Do you ever think about him?"

"Oh, all the time. I think about the good times, mostly. I have a theory about those memories, too, and this is the perfect night to tell it."

"What?"

"Well, you see all those fireflies flickering out there and you see all those bright stars up there?"

"I see."

"Well, I think that whenever a happy moment occurs and a memory is created, the fireflies come along to carry it away. That's when they light up. They bring it up to the sky and it's stored in the stars. Then, those memories are flown back down at night, while we sleep; the light is dropped off then; the memory. They are given as dreams to those who most need them."

"I like that theory."

"You know it's a secret though, right?'

"Why?"

"Well, if we let on that we know, then they may not drop those dreams off to us. That's why they only visit people when they are unconscious or just waking up or just falling asleep. Then, they can't get caught. I think they like to be anonymous dream-givers. Besides, once you're fully awake, wouldn't you want to be yourself? Who wants to walk around stuck in the memory of somebody else's life just because the dream didn't have a chance to escape before you woke up?"

"Who do you think gets the dreams?"

"Oh, I don't know. I'd like to think that they go to people who can't experience them for themselves. Maybe a little girl somewhere dreams the memory of a candy maker and she can really taste the sweets. Or maybe some kid who lives in the freezing cold tundra gets the memory of one of us down here in the good old A.Z. and he's warmed all night long."

"Or maybe a boy who can't move dreams of playing ball?" asked Cooper innocently.

"Sure, Cooper," answered his mom after a short pause and a warm glance. "So, what memories have you added to the mix up there? You must have some happy ones?"

"Mom, I have a lot with you!" he assured her.

"I hope so, hon," she said.

"I do have one of Dad, too. Well, more than one, but one that's my favorite."

"What is it?" she asked.

"Well," he began, and then stopped. "Hmm . . ." He smiled and sighed deeply.

"It's okay," said Cooper's mom. "That one can be between you and the fireflies."

"I don't mind, Mom. I tell you everything. It's the boats. I remember when Dad would sail his model boats. It was fun."

"I remember those old boats, Coop. I guess that's why you like to keep that one up on your shelf in the bedroom?" she wondered aloud.

"Yeah. I like to look at it. But, it's just one memory and I bet we'll keep them fireflies super busy tomorrow carrying all those new memories to the stars when you get married."

"I bet we will, Bud. I bet we will."

April and Cooper sat quietly for awhile longer on the porch swing with their heads balanced against one another, staring at the stars and the fireflies and soaking in the cool, night air on their last night home as just the two of them. Then, April put Cooper into his chair, pushed him down the hallway, and—after bedtime exercises—tucked him neatly into his bed, with the curtains opened and the window cracked, of course.

Chapter 9

Model Ships

The wedding went off without a hitch and, after a small weekend vacation for Derek and Cooper's mom during which Aunt May stayed at the house to care for Cooper, Derek moved in and they all became a real family. In no time at all, Christmas was upon the happy new family of three that was added to by the extended family of Aunt May and Uncle Harry for one last joint holiday before their move.

They played Christmas music on the radio and Cooper watched them all dance and laugh with one another. Aunt May even danced his wheelchair about the room to the tune of "Jingle Bell Rock". Derek read Christmas stories and they all called all sorts of friends and relatives throughout the festivities. They even had a small fire in the living room fireplace that, the rest of the year, was used only to hold a decorative candelabrum. Cooper's mom threw some cinnamon sticks and orange peels into the flames so that the whole house smelled of holiday spices.

In the morning, the whole family cut and hung up paper snowflakes. They played with them when the music turned to such tunes as *White Christmas*, for—in Southern Arizona—even Uncle Harry had yet to witness a snowy holiday, and he'd been there his whole life. They had a game every year of pulling down the crafted white papers each time a Christmas song mentioned snow and then they would toss them into the holiday fire. The few snowflakes that they made rarely lasted the night. If any did last, they would be packed away with the Christmas decorations and used the next year to help start the new holiday fire.

For dinner, Derek had boiled a ham so tender that Cooper got to have some real pieces besides just his pureed version! He also had squash and rice and hot cider fed to him. It was as though Cooper was no different than the rest of them. He even enjoyed pumpkin pie, minus the crust; but, who likes the crust, anyway? Also, from his stocking, he got to enjoy a Santa-shaped piece of fudge.

The gifts seemed to last all day and night that Christmas. Nicholas stopped by to give Cooper a special joystick, just like the one he'd used at the friend's house. It was for a new baseball video game and he promised to come play every week until his real little league started up in spring and he had to practice with them. Cooper gave him a new yo-yo with a DVD full of tricks for him to practice.

Aunt May and Uncle Harry gave Cooper a travel voucher to come visit them in Washington State. He was so excited! Cooper gave them a picture book of Arizona to take along to their new home.

To his mom, Cooper and Derek had picked out a collection of some really great garage sale treasures for her to refurbish and sell in her online business. Plus, Derek gave her a Christmas dress that she loved so much; she changed into it right away and wore it all day long, even when everybody else was still in their pajamas from the morning.

Derek received some books on physical therapy from Aunt May and Uncle Harry and some of his own embroidered household items from Cooper and April, to match things they already had.

Cooper's mom had given Cooper all new bedding. It was the colors of the Arizona Diamondbacks and came with a matching new wall clock for his room that would play music. The clock could be programmed as an alarm to go off at a time that could be set using Cooper's own voice instead of using buttons!

When it came time to receive Derek's gift, Cooper wasn't overly excited as his mom opened it for him while he watched. Every year, it was more audio books and usually those books ended up becoming assignments before long. This year's package was bigger than usual, so surely the listening was long and probably boring. When she finished removing the paper, though, Cooper's jaw dropped.

"I hope it's okay," said Derek. He took the unwrapped gift from April and sat face to face with Cooper. It was a model sailing ship, much like those that his father used to sail with him on the pond in the park. "I'm not your Dad, Coop, and I'll never try to replace

him. But, I want you to know that I will be the best person I can
be for you and for your mother."

"But I can't push these anymore," Cooper replied and he
immediately felt stupid for it. Derek was talking to him heart-to-heart
and he was focused on the small model ship complete with sails of
real canvas.

"I know," said Derek, not at all offended. "It has a remote, now.
It's not the same. But, it can go across a pond without our help and
we can enjoy launching it and watching it together. What do you
think?"

"I'd like that," Cooper said sincerely. Then, something happened
that he didn't expect. Derek kissed him on the forehead, just like he'd
dreamed when he was Danny Mills, The Wonder Kid and Danny's
dad was affectionate with his son after the championship win. He
smiled back and felt his cheeks burn with blushing.

When Aunt May and Uncle Harry left for the night, it was a
long, tearful goodbye that seemed to never end. Every time they
all hugged and kissed and said farewell, they'd begin all over again
with talks about when they'd all see one another next and whether
or not everybody was taken care of, his Aunt and Uncle for the trip
and his family for the care of himself. It was some forty-five minutes
of hard crying. Cooper hated crying. His nose would run as heavily
as his tears would fall and he'd feel like he had an awful cold. He
got a hold of himself so that he wouldn't become so congested that
his mom would have to hook him up to the ventilator that night.
On the true, final goodbye, the rain started to fall and it was even
sadder to watch them drive away in the middle of a rare, Arizona
storm.

Afterward, Cooper, his mom and Derek came in and just sat
quietly by the fire talking about the wonderful day. They all sipped
hot cocoa and stared at their presents. Cooper felt himself dozing.
His head was heavy with the excitement of the day and the cool of
the night.

That night, Cooper's mom and Derek both tucked him into bed.
They put the new model ship on his dresser across the room. He
would have Derek build a second shelf, eventually. That way, both
ships could have a place of honor where he could watch them on the
special shelves across from his bed. Tonight, he was so full of peaceful
joy for the day that he didn't feel he needed the extra view just yet.

"I should pull the shade down," said April. "All that rain out there is sure to keep you up." Cooper's mom pulled down the shade and the entire thing accidentally fell. "Oh dear. I hate it when it does that!"

"It's okay, Mom." Cooper assured her.

"Well, let me close the curtains at least," she said.

"No, don't. Please. I like it opened," Coop said quietly.

"Well, I'll fix it for you, Bud, but not tonight." She rolled up the fallen shade.

The bat and yo-yo had fallen over when the shade came down and Cooper couldn't see them. He didn't say a word, but while his mom rolled up the shade and set it aside in his closet, Derek balanced the bat back up against the window ledge and placed the yo-yo on the nightstand next to the lamp in exactly the same positions they had been in before. Cooper gave a knowing, closed-lipped half grin to his step-dad. Both his mom and Derek kissed him on the forehead and wished him a Merry Christmas night of dreams, then left the room.

Dreams, thought Cooper. *Who needs them on a day like today?* His mom had slept him propped up somewhat tonight so he was able to smile at the model ship from his father that rested on the shelf across from him. He sighed a happy, albeit, slightly congested breath and drifted off to sleep.

*   *   *

Cooper looked down at his legs and feet. They were short, very short. He bent them up, then playfully hopped up onto them and began to run around a small pond. He could hear his own laughter ringing in his ears.

"Wait up, Dad!" he called. "I wanna see! I wanna see!"

"Come on, little man, keep up. We have to do it from this side to catch the wind. Come on over!"

The man knelt down at one side of the park's small pond. A very young Cooper ran right to his side and plopped down dramatically next to his dad. He looked into the water and saw his own reflection, that of a four-year-old Cooper, staring back.

"Now what?" he asked.

"Now we launch it," said Cooper's dad. He was holding a small model sailing ship and he set it gently on the surface of the water at its edge. "Go ahead, you do it."

"How?" said the younger Ridge.

"Just a gentle push. You can do it. There's just enough wind here today that it should pick it up the rest of the way and we can collect it on the other side."

"What if it doesn't work?"

"It will. I promise," said Cooper's dad.

Cooper pushed the small model ship gently with his pudgy, toddler hand. The ship began a slow drift.

"It's barely moving," whined Cooper.

"You're right!" said his dad. "It needs a little help. Blow!"

Cooper and his dad flopped onto their bellies along the grassy side of the park pond. The two laughed heartily while they puffed their cheeks out and blew repeatedly against the tiny sails.

"It's not enough, my boy! Bring in the motors!"

"What motors, Dad?"

"Splash! Go on, now! Splash!"

Cooper put his hands in the water and fluttered them about toward the stern of the little model. Caught up in the laughing fun he was sharing with his dad, he turned his splashes from the ship to his dad. "Gotcha, Daddy!" he giggled as he splashed again and again at the man.

"Oh yeah?" he joked back. "Well, you know what I gotta do, then!" he exclaimed. With that, Mr. Ridge scooped a handful of water toward his young son.

The water splashed through the air and it hit Cooper in the face all at once cold and quick and wet. He flinched.

*　*　*

Cooper snapped awake in an instant, feeling sure he had just been doused in ice water. His whole body jerked in reaction. Then, a warm tickle in his ear and he lay motionless again.

It couldn't be. Did he really move just then? It had to be the dream. It must just have felt more real because it was a dream from his own past; a dream of a time that he had spent with his own dad. That's all it was. It had to be. But, why then, were his toes out of the covers? Surely his mom and Derek had tucked them in. Or did they? He looked down at his exposed foot and panted heavily through his stuffy nose and dry mouth. If he could have felt his own heart, he was sure it must have been thumping wildly. His eyes teared up with exhilarated confusion.

He turned his head toward the window. The rain was still falling down. That's what it must have been. Rain from the window splashed his face in his sleep. And his foot? Well, Derek wasn't used to the nighttime routine. He must not have tucked in Cooper's feet is all. Or maybe when the shade fell, it bumped the bedding and pulled the quilt off of his toes. That had to be it.

Cooper methodically forced his breathing to slow and he blinked away the moisture welling up in the bottom of his alert eyes. Finally, he let his lids heavily droop shut; the last sight Cooper saw before he slipped back into a dreamless sleep was that of a small firefly flying out the open crack of his bedroom window and up to the stars above.

Chapter 10

Cotton and Snow

The New Year brought with it a terrible head cold that drained from Cooper's nose and throat straight back into his ears. The ache throbbed so deeply that Cooper cried in pain. So, a home doctor's visit led to some medicine and ear drops.

Derek even let Cooper miss lessons for a couple of days and watch movies instead, right from his bed. Cooper's mom brought his meal shakes into his room for him. Mostly, he slept, but the ear infection just didn't seem to want to go away.

"I should never have left his window open that night; and with no shade, to boot!" Cooper's mom frustratingly ranted to Derek down the hall while Cooper listened.

"What difference could the shade make, April?" he asked trying to calm her down. "Stop blaming yourself."

"It's just that you know I can't sleep when he doesn't feel well," she went on.

"It's not your fault. Look, I'll even fix the shade; promise. April, the bottom line is that all kids get colds," he reassured his wife.

"Maybe. But, most of those kids can at least blow their noses. I get so worried about his breathing, Derek, even when I do suction his nose out with the bulb. I could put him on the ventilator, but the doctor says he doesn't need it right now. Plus, Coop can't stand the thing. He feels like it's digressing or something. I work very hard keeping things clean and safe around here so that he doesn't get sick. I just hate it is all," she grumbled.

"Aren't the drops helping at all?" he asked.

"I think they're just draining right out of his ears," she replied. "He has to sleep propped up to help him breathe, so the drops just stream right back out, down his jaw line; make more mess than they're worth. Maybe if they stayed in his ears a little longer, they'd actually help to make him better."

"Not a big deal, April, really. Just put cotton in his ears at night. Then, he can sleep propped up and the medicine won't drain," he offered.

"I guess that could work," she sighed. "It better. This is why I hate for him to be sick. And this is just basically a cold! I don't know what we'll ever do if he gets truly ill."

"Well, I know *you* won't sleep for all of your worrying," he said.

"Can you blame me?" she asked.

"No, I can't. It's one of the things I love about you, after all," Derek finished.

So, that night, when Cooper was cleaned up for bed, his mom went to work to make him better. She fluffed up the pillows he'd been laying on for most of the last two days and she gave him his medicine and ear drops, then propped him up and put cotton into his ears to keep the liquid from draining; now, the medicine could do its job.

"I'm going to close your window, Bud," April said as she began to shut it tight.

"Don't, Mom," Cooper begged.

"But, Coop—"

"No, don't. It's not rainy or even that cool. I like the air," he continued to plead.

"Oh, alright. But, you call me in if you get stuffy, okay?" she said with a worried expression.

"I will," Cooper promised.

"And I mean the very second, Coop, got it?" she pointed her finger in warning.

"Yes ma'am," Cooper half-laughed.

Cooper wasn't really tired since he'd slept so much lately. So, he mostly laid there thinking. He turned his head toward his open window and smiled drearily at his bat and yo-yo. He turned his head to look next to his bed at the small lamp on the nightstand. It was left on a low setting while he was sick in case his mom or Derek needed to check on him in the night. He looked at both of his ships; the one from Derek on the dresser across the room and the one from his dad on the shelf. He looked also over his bed at his new clock radio on the wall. He had programmed it to go off at 7:00am, the same as his mother's, and it would play music from his favorite radio station which was not at all the same as his mother's. Cooper was bored just laying there wide awake. Tonight, he actually longed for a dream.

It seemed hours had passed. Cooper's time finally grew dull enough that he began to yawn and wearily flutter his dry, dozy eyes open and shut.

Then, he saw above him two, little, flickering lights. Fireflies had made their way into his room again. He looked toward them deliriously and was unsure if he was imagining things or miniscule sounds were also floating about in the air of his room.

> *"Is this the right boy?" asked the first.*
> *"That's him. He's almost ready," said a second.*
> *"He needs to be completely asleep?" the first questioned.*
> *"No, just mostly. It's okay when he's just waking or just falling asleep; but no coming or going when he's totally conscious. You'd have to wait for him to drift off again."*
> *"Got it," the first tiny voice finished as one of the flickering lights flew out of the window.*

Surely, his exhaustion and the medicines, or maybe the plugged ears, made him hear those high, buzzing whispers that weren't really there. Perhaps it was just sounds from outside his window; the rustling of the trees or the occasional passing of a car down a neighborhood road.

"I'm going to go check on him, Derek, and change the cotton in his ears," he heard his mom say from down the hall. Her voice was crisp and clear, unlike the miniscule sounds he had heard just before.

"Okay, but I tell you, he's fine," Derek comforted her like a parent.

"I know, I know. But, I have to check," she said.

As Cooper heard her slippered feet sweeping down the hallway toward his room, the remaining small firefly rose to the little lamp next his bed and rested in its glow, almost completely camouflaged by the light casted onto the nightstand.

Cooper blinked away the sleep for a moment when his mom entered the room.

"Are you still up, Bud?" she asked. "Can't sleep?"

"Just not tired," he responded, through a hollow yawn.

"Really," she laughed lightly. "Well, try. Just close your eyes and pretend and before you know it, you'll be out. I just came to change the cotton in your ears," April said as she pulled out the small balls of fluff from his ears.

Cooper smiled tiredly at his mom and then allowed the night to take over again, closing his heavy eyes. He heard April leave the room. Before she returned, his infected ear tickled lightly. He slit open his eyes groggily, in a half-sleep and looked toward his lamp. He couldn't see the firefly at all even though he was sure it had been there before. *Couldn't be,* he thought sleepily.

While his mind floated into dreams, Cooper allowed the sounds of his mother's returning to his room melt into his nighttime imaginings. He felt her put fresh cotton into his ears, but he was already fast asleep. His eyes were rapidly moving in a dreamscape nothing like the room in which he actually lay.

*   *   *

"Good hit, son," said the man across from the small barn where Cooper stood with a bat. A white square was drawn with chalk on the red, wooden planks behind him.

"I think it's gonna be a great season, Dad," Cooper said. "Matt's got an awesome new curve *and* he's still got a wicked fastball. I think we're going to take the championship for the fifth straight year."

"Only your third, though, young one. Besides, you have to make the team first. I don't want you getting all full of yourself and thinking that just because you were the MVP last year, you have an automatic in. You have to try out just like the rest of the players. That's why we're practicing."

"It's almost two months to tryouts, Dad."

"Good! That gives us plenty of time, then," the man responded as he threw the ball hard into the white square behind Cooper. "Strike one!"

"No fair. You caught me off guard."

"Then, put your guard up, son!"

"All right, ole man! Try me," Cooper joked.

"Who you calling old, little tyke?" exclaimed the man as he threw another perfect pitch toward his son.

Cooper swung hard at the ball and felt the impact of it against the bat buzz down the Louisville Slugger and vibrate in his wrists. "That's who!" he laughed. "That one is long gone!"

"That it is!" said the man. "Here. Catch!" he called as he threw a solid white ball hard at Cooper's head.

"Hey!" he shouted, ducking quickly away from the impact. It turned out to be only snow, Cooper noticed as it splatted against the side of the barn. Of course his dad could never throw a ball at him. "That was a cheap shot, Dad."

"Gotcha! That's what you get for calling me *ole man*, Danny Mills!"

Cooper refused to open his eyes even though he was just called Danny Mills. He could feel himself fighting to stay asleep. He could feel the dream struggling to get away. He squinted his eyes tightly shut, willing the fantasy to stay. *No*, he thought. *I want the dream. Ignore the name. Don't wake up. Don't wake up!*

The two men tossed some bare-handed snowballs at one another. One struck Cooper in the shoulder and split open, spraying snow into his ear.

"Hey!" he reached up to brush off his ear.

*　　*　　*

Cooper snapped awake and simultaneously the cold sprayed ear from his dream became the infected one from his real life and filled with a warm tickle.

Cooper looked at the window and saw a firefly making a quick and crooked escape as though it had been trapped in a jar from which there was no exit and it finally was able to flee. But, that firefly wasn't the only one with an escape plan. For, Cooper looked down at his hand—the one with which, in the dream, he had brushed off his snow-dusted ear. A cotton ball lay in that hand. Cooper had pulled it out; he was sure of it, and for the first time, he understood everything.

Chapter 11

Letting the Dreams Go By

"How'd you sleep, Bud?" Cooper's mom said to him in the morning after they both woke up to their alarms.

"Fine."

"What's this?" she asked when she spotted the cotton in her son's hand.

"It fell out," he lied. There was no need to talk to her about what he knew or how the cotton came to be in his hand. Soon, he hoped, it wouldn't matter.

"Oh. Sorry about that. I must not have done a good job at putting it in last night. I was a little tired, too. How do your ears feel today?"

"I think the trick worked. Cotton is a miracle cure, Mom!" he smiled wryly at her. He had barely slept after his discovery, so his words sounded tired and lazy.

"You still seem a little groggy. Were you up again after I checked on you?" she wondered as she brushed his forehead with the back of her hand and adjusted his covers and pillows much as a nurse would do for a hospital patient.

"A little," he fibbed a second time.

"Well, I'll tell Derek to hold off one more day before he starts up with your lessons. I'll bring you in a nice warm breakfast drink and I'll wrap your throat in a warm towel and I'll even wheel the DVD player in here again so that you can watch some movies, sound good?'

"Sounds great!" said Cooper.

"Which movies today?" April questioned her son.

"Um . . ." he thought for a moment. "How about *The Bad News Bears* and *Angels in the Outfield?*"

"Oh, I see. It's a theme today. Sure, hon. You rest up and I'll be right back."

Cooper enjoyed the lazy day recovering from his cold and earache. Derek sat in a chair next to his bed and watched the baseball movies with him. Then, they listened to an audio book about Shoeless Joe Jackson and his banned team of players. They talked about when Spring Training was to start for the Arizona Diamondbacks and who they thought would be benched or step up to the plate this year. Derek promised he'd bring Cooper to a game, again—and he wouldn't even have to keep stats. April brought them both breakfast and lunch in the bedroom. It was a quiet, fun day. Tomorrow the routine of life would begin again. With a private new hope alive in Cooper's heart, though, he faced even the most mundane of days and doings with a knowing smile and peaceful optimism. He was secretly waiting for something else . . . something more.

Regarding his education, Cooper now had the added benefit of being able to relax and joke a little more with Derek . . . err . . . *Mr. Lowell.* For, during his studies, he was still to refer to his step dad by his teaching title. Oh, Cooper still had to meet his teacher's strict standards, but as long as he did so, the school day atmosphere remained light and even, sometimes, fun.

Mr. Lowell had grown used to doing the physical therapy exercises and the autos with Cooper. He was different than both Aunt May and his mom. Aunt May was always all business. Cooper's mom was always kind and gentle. Mr. Lowell tried to be both, but was not comfortable enough yet to be either. He sometimes seemed nervous and he couldn't always make eye contact with Cooper. Each time grew easier, though. Cooper enjoyed being the one who had to instruct his instructor whenever Mr. Lowell forgot how to set an auto routine or perform a particular stretch. He was good with taking vitals, though. It seemed Mr. Lowell was most comfortable with something as solid as numbers. One day, he commented that all of Cooper's "stats" were looking good, so they must be doing well together.

*   *   *

That night, Cooper dreamed of going to the middle school with a whole staff of teachers; somebody different for each subject and for P.E. He set up his very own locker with pictures of all of his favorite baseball players. It felt real. He could feel the cold metal of the locker and hear the clicks of his new combination lock. It's not the dream he wanted. He was secretly waiting for something else . . . something more. Cooper let it pass peacefully away from a warmed and tickled ear and his sleep became dreamless again. He remained aware of his surroundings even as he continued to slumber.

*   *   *

Nicholas came over once a week to practice yo-yo or play video games. Sometimes, the two boys would watch a movie with one another. One week, he brought Beaches along and both boys practiced training the dog with their yo-yos. Nicholas went through an entire pocketful of treats!

*   *   *

That night, Cooper dreamed he was taking a run with Beaches through the neighborhood. He waved to every neighbor he passed and each waved back in turn. It felt real. He could feel his feet pounding the sidewalk. He could hear the panting of Beaches. It's not the dream he wanted. He was secretly waiting for something else . . . something more. Cooper let it pass peacefully away from a warmed and tickled ear and his sleep became dreamless again. He remained aware of his surroundings even as he continued to slumber.

*   *   *

He had even more one-on-one time with his mom since Derek became part of the family. Because Derek was always around, his mom didn't have to go out to be with her husband, so her home time could be spent with her son. One day, she woke him early and cleaned him up. April put her son into his chair and they went for a walk through the neighborhood for the annual community garage sale. She often found some of her best treasures for her business here, and Cooper loved to help spot them. The ice cream truck stopped across the way from one of the sales and Cooper watched and listened as a young boy ran excitedly to the window and was then treated to a sno-cone by his mother.

*　　*　　*

That night, Cooper dreamed he was walking through his neighborhood for the annual garage sale with his mom at his side. The ice cream truck stopped for them and she treated both to sno-cones. It felt real. He could feel the wetness of shaved ice against his lips. He could taste the sweet, blue syrup on his tongue. It's not the dream he wanted. He was secretly waiting for something else . . . something more. Cooper let it pass peacefully away from a warmed and tickled ear and his sleep became dreamless again. He remained aware of his surroundings even as he continued to slumber.

*　　*　　*

It was March; a perfect Saturday morning. The sun was shining in the crisp, blue sky and the scarce breezes were light and cool. The Ridge-Lowell family of three got up nice and early and had breakfast together in the kitchen. Then, it was time for a "guys' day out", according to Derek.

"We'll be home about five, April" he said to his wife before kissing her goodbye and loading Cooper and himself into their special, handicapped van to go for a drive.

"Where we going?" Cooper asked.

"We're going out for lunch and to some stores. First, though, I'm taking you to watch Nicholas try out for the little league team. He's too young for the official team, but they have a junior team that practices right before the older boys and that's where most of the county-sponsored team ends up coming from in the long run. I thought you'd enjoy watching them. Plus, the primary team will be there as well, so there'll be a lot of boys your own age," Derek finished.

The two had a wonderful day; a father-son outing of sorts. They did all of the things Derek had promised.

Cooper had the idea that Derek, or maybe Nicholas, had possibly primed the older kids about how to treat him. Many of the boys Cooper's age had stopped by him on the side of the bleachers to say hello and almost none of them seemed to notice the fact that he was in a wheelchair. It was a little obvious, really. Nonetheless, it was sweet in its own way.

He and Derek ate at a new restaurant called *Soup's On!* which was nothing but soups, breads and salads. Cooper had a huge selection of brothy meals from which to choose. Then, the men walked through a sports store and looked at all of the neat things. In another store, they tried to find another good video game, but they couldn't find any that worked as well for Cooper as those that Nicholas had always managed to discover and share over the years. He would have to find a way to thank him again for obviously searching so hard for his friend, Cooper. At the day's end, just before returning home, they got ice cream.

Then, for the drive home, Derek and Cooper discussed all of the great players and not-so-great players that they'd witnessed trying out for little league. Thankfully, both agreed that Nicholas was one of the best. Cooper wouldn't have to pretend he felt that way when the subject arose as it surely would. Nicholas deserved it because he'd been practicing often and hard. Cooper had himself been able to watch him several times.

That night, Cooper was tucked into his bed as exhausted as he imagined an almost thirteen-year-old could possibly feel. With much difficulty, he forced himself to remain aware of his surroundings even as he drifted into slumber. There was a dream he wanted and he was secretly waiting for something else . . . something more.

Chapter 12

The One He Was Waiting For

Cooper never felt himself fall asleep. He never felt the first tickle in his ear. It was almost as though he had floated out into the batting cage on that practice field, much like the misty fog that was settled upon it now.

Cooper took a deep breath of the wet, early spring air. He looked down at himself in the baseball uniform, a Washington Wonderboys scrub outfit. He looked at his own hands and feet and he knew himself. This was the one he'd been waiting for. Cooper was sure of it.

He wanted to revel in the moment of the dream, but he had to hold onto his senses. He would need them soon. His heart began to beat hard with anticipation. Would his plan even work or was he as crazy as he was crippled for believing in it? He knew what his cue would be. Cooper forced himself to remain calm in his sleep to keep the dream. He must not wake yet. He was waiting for something else . . . something more. It was a name. That would be his cue and only then, when he willed his entire self to make the impossible happen, would he know that he could.

Don't think about it, he told himself. *Be in the dream. Be in the dream and wait for your cue.*

It was pretty cool out today, and overcast, too. Nicer temperatures didn't usually arrive in his western Washington State hometown until about May. The wind was straight off the Pacific which was not a good thing this time of year. The Saturday morning air was damp and thick and it was hard to keep warm, even with his jacket snapped all the way up over his practice uniform. He pulled his cap down tight over his forehead, shading his eyes against the cold and blinking away the wind-caused tears. He sniffled lightly and shrugged his shoulders, stretching his head and neck in a back and forth rolling motion. He yawned widely. Cooper stood up jumpingly, then paced about so he could warm up his muscles at least as much as his nerves.

His turn would come, but right now it was time to watch the pitching and none other than his best pal Matt was on the mound. He wished his dad would get back soon to watch this. He had dropped Coop off to run and grab some coffee for himself and hot chocolate for his son. Cooper wanted to hold the drink more than to drink it, he thought as he balled up his hands into fists and stuffed them into his jacket pockets, shaking off the morning shivers all the while. Others on the bench were huddled up, but Cooper knew he had to get psyched for the try-out and not let the hour of day, or the weather of it, keep him down.

"Not bad, Hill, not bad at all!" said an approving coach with a deep, slow nod toward the mound. "You've been working on that curve ball, haven't you?"

"Yes, Sir!" Matt grinned back proudly.

"But, how's that fastball faring since you're giving all your attention to the new curve?"

"Hope that catcher's mitt's got extra padding!" he confidently smirked. He didn't look anything like the Matt who was shifting back and forth on his feet in the championship game last season. Cooper smiled at his friend out there some fifty-four feet away and shook his head laughingly.

Coach looked to his Wonder Kid and chuckled as if to say, "*Well, he's your friend.*"

For a moment, he thought his cue was coming and he nearly awoke but the coach just dropped his head and turned back toward Matt. Cooper breathed slow and deep and allowed his eyelids to be thick and heavy.

"Alright, Matt, let's see it!" said the man in charge.

"That was it!"

"Very funny, Mr. Hill! You're fast, but you ain't that good!"

"Just joshing with ya!" the pitcher laughed. He was in great spirits. Cooper actually felt bad for the poor couple of guys that came to try out for pitcher. They would never be the go-to guy so long as his pal was still around. Although, there was nothing shotty about being the relief pitcher on a championship team, either; that is, as long as you didn't mind sitting out five of six innings per game.

Coop's best friend barreled in pitch after pitch. Only one ball the entire time; all the rest were spot on, and fast! All of the batters who tried out with Matt on the mound begged for another try with somebody else throwing a few for them. Finally, Coach just broke down and told Matt, "You made the team, already, Hill. Now, could you lighten up on the new kids?" For, nobody could get a hit off on Matt Hill if he didn't want it.

"Glad you're on my team, man," Cooper laughed out to him.

"You mean *my* team, Wonder Kid! You still gotta make it!" his friend joked back.

Once again, he almost awoke with the anticipation of a name . . . that didn't come. His ear grew warm for a moment, but it didn't tickle. He calmed his heart. The dream, that had grown blurry for the shortest of moments, returned with full clarity. *Keep your senses,* thought Cooper. *Keep the dream, but keep your senses.*

The fog had burned off or risen above the field for the most part as the Saturday carried on and a hazy, spring sunshine flooded the anxious auditioners holed up in the cage like cattle waiting to be driven. This year's cattle made a longer list than ever before. There's something bad to be said about having a great sports reputation: *Everybody* wants to be a part of the team! So, from the youngest eligible to the oldest eligible (not to mention those who tried to sneak in who were not yet or no longer eligible), there were players who had never even held a bat or ball stepping up to the plate or out to the field or onto the mound. This made the early started morning drag to nearly noon before Coach had narrowed down the field to actual serious contenders.

If there's something good to be said about the reputation, though, it's that all the best also came out to join the Washington Wonderboys. This year's competition amongst the potential players was fierce and the team would be great for it! Keeping warm was certainly no longer a problem once Cooper began moving around against his possible teammates.

Cooper didn't mind so much that there were some good hitters. It was the fielders that had him worried. He had been hoping to move up to shortstop this year and some of the older boys had such speed out there that he wasn't sure he'd be able to hold his own. His dad, who had returned at some point into the try-out to cheer on his son and his son's best friend, assured Cooper that it wouldn't be a problem for The Wonder Kid!

Cooper's number was called for speed trials and he hung in with the best of the players running the bases. He opted not to throw any pitches. Even if he could keep up with his friend, which he couldn't, he would never want to challenge Matt's position on the team. When it was his turn to bat, he was quietly grateful that he was pitched to by a boy who would probably make a good relief pitcher, but was nowhere near as tough as his friend. He got off a fly to an uncovered position and a grounder that led to a double.

"You're doing great, son," said Cooper's dad with a strong, squeezing pat on the shoulder when he'd returned from the batting portion of the try-out. "Just one thing left, you'll do just fine!" He pulled down his son's cap affectionately. His dad's eyes had such a gleam of joy.

Cooper waited for something more . . . for a name. But, it didn't come. He squeezed his eyes tighter and forced his heavy breathing to slow in order to calm his heart. His cue would come soon enough.

The two waited patiently through some of the best and worst players they had ever seen on display for the Wonderboys' coach. Matt stuck around to support his friend even after he left the mound to give some other kids a chance to attempt to line up behind him on the roster.

Finally, it was Cooper's turn to practice fielding. He went deep first. Then, he had to throw from each base to each of the others. Finally, he was near the baseline as shortstop. Ball after ball was tossed his way high, low, on the ground, to either side and every other which way possible. Time and again, the ball didn't get past Cooper. He dirtied that uniform through and through and sacrificed his body for the ball the same as he would have for a real game. His dad in the foreground was a blur of fists in the air, jumping about and, once, hugging his pal, Matt after Cooper had stretched his long body out particularly far to catch a ball just as it was about to bounce in the dirt.

When all was said and done, Cooper had only missed one ball thrown his way. The next person closest had missed four. It would have been a pure injustice for Cooper not to have made the team. They would be hearing the results, next.

Cooper forced his breathing once again to slow. He couldn't believe the dream, the memory, lasted this long. Cooper knew there was no way his cue wouldn't come now. Coach was going to read off the roster and that would bring the name for certain; that would bring the cue. That would be his chance to prove to himself that this was real. He saw the blurriness of the dream as his heart began beat hard in his chest. He barely clung on to the drowsy state necessary to keep the nightscape rolling, but it was enough. He needed to be alert and asleep at the same time.

"Alright, boys. Great job, today," began Coach. "Now, when I call your name, come on up next to me and you will be my starters. The rest of you that still remain here are on the team, but you're bench for now. That could change as the season goes on. So, don't go getting soft on me or walking off. Hard work will pay on the Washington Wonderboys. That's a promise."

Cooper breathed deeply in his bed and in his dream.

"Matt Hill, Pitcher!" said the coach.

Next, Coach read off the name of the catcher, 1st base, 2nd base, 3rd base . . .

"And for shortstop, we have a new starter this year," he began.

Cooper took a long, slow, calming breath.

"Danny Mills, come on over!" he called to Cooper.

*   *   *

That was it! In an instant flash; a second of time at most, squeezing his eyes shut as tight as possible, Cooper willed every bit of his dream self to come to life and he slapped both of his hands up fast and hard against the sides of his head before the different name had time to snap him from his imaginings. "WAKE UP!" he shouted boldly out loud to himself and then he forced his eyes open wide.

His ears were hot and tingling, but there was no tickle. Cooper panted hard, his hands still tight against his ears; so tight they throbbed in the vacuum of humming sounds around him. The world was a muffled ringing. He held his eyes open as largely as possible in the dim night glow in his room. His gaze raced about, taking in all that was around him and the waking world was coming into focus. He saw the model ship across from his bed and he felt his own heart beating rapidly in his chest. His hands were on his head. He dare not move another millimeter. Cooper continued to visually scan all that was around him, willing himself to believe that he was in his room and no longer in his dream.

"Cooper!" called April in a midnight panic stumbling down the hallway. "Cooper, what is it?" she shouted as she threw back the door, entered his room and rolled the knob-like light switch near the entrance to turn on the overhead light in his room to its full, maximum brightness. She looked at her son and gasped a stifled scream. "Oh my God," she finally managed meekly.

Cooper turned his eyes toward his mother who still stood frozen in the doorway, her own hands held against her dropped jaw and mouth; a look of combined panic and exhilaration upon her face.

He kept his hands clapped tightly against the sides of his head and breathily . . . *shakily* . . . trembled out the question, "Mom . . . Mom, am I awake?" Cooper's eyes watered and he lay still except for his wildly shifting eyes still taking in the reality of his setting.

April wordlessly and quakily shook her head for a moment, seemingly unable to form words. Finally, as she stared wide-open-mouthed at her son, she stuttered a reply of, "I don't . . . I don't know. I don't know if *I* am, Bud."

"What's going on?" a yawning Derek mumbled as he clunked down the hallway toward his family. Derek entered the room and looked at Cooper, suddenly completely awake, and then he froze in the same way as his wife, at her side in the wooden frame of the thrown open door.

"I'm awake," said Cooper again and again. "I'm awake. I'm awake." In an almost trance-like state, Cooper did the unthinkable in front of his mom and step-dad. Keeping his hands on his ears, he slowly lifted his body away from the pillows. The action was so slow; it looked almost magical; supernatural, like when a magician makes a lying woman rise above a stage. Then, Cooper turned his legs and *sat* on the edge of his bed looking at April and Derek. "I'm awake," he said again as unwilling tears began to stream out of his eyes and he blinked them out repeatedly to rain continuously down his cheekbones.

In his head, Cooper played back the voices he'd heard over his bed months ago.

> *"He needs to be completely asleep?" the first questioned.*
> *"No, just mostly. It's okay when he's just waking or just falling asleep; but no coming or going when he's totally conscious. You'd have to wait for him to drift off again."*
> *"Got it."*

Got it, Cooper thought to himself as a reassurance.

"I'm awake," he said through rapid breaths and a fluttering heartbeat. His tone was strong, as though he were giving an order of some kind. He stared glossy-eyed at his awed mom and step-dad. Then, he swallowed hard, hoping against hope that he would be right as he closed his eyes, lips trembling in a panicked cry. Very slowly, deliberately and cautiously, Cooper lowered his twittering hands from the sides of his head. The blood in his arms was buzzing. Then, he reopened his eyes like slow-rising suns and resumed calming breaths, still methodically scanning his surroundings.

"No tickle," he said with a broken voice through his throat; lumped with emotion. "I'm awake. I'm awake," he bawled now openly.

Finally and silently—except for an exhale that seemed to have been on hold for a decade—April dropped her hands from her mouth and drifted floatingly to her son. She kneeled before him on the floor in front of the bed and, after putting her hands on his cheeks with a transparent need to feel that he was real, she stared into his own moist eyes. Then, she sobbingly wrapped her arms around him, weeping in his lap as though she were the child who could not speak in this overwhelming moment.

"Oh my God," said Derek at last. He ran clumsily over and plopped beside Cooper on the bed. All pretenses of masculinity melted away as he tearfully and tightly—as though holding them from falling away—slid and squeezed one arm each around his wife and step-son. "Yes. You're awake. We're all awake, but it feels like a dream, Coop. It feels like a dream."

Finally, the family of three, in a private time when the world seemed *fixed,* was broken down into wails of grateful disbelief.

Chapter 13

Being Awake

The wordless weeping shared by the three went on for some unmeasured time. It was still dark outside, but none of them cared about the hour. Cooper's trickling teardrops finally stopped flowing and he looked up at the new clock over his bed. It was 12:28am.

Gently, he took Derek's arm down from around his shoulders and he pushed his hands deliberately against his mom's shoulders, lifting her carefully off of his lap. Every move he made gave him confidence to try more.

He unattached himself from the tubes he'd seen his mother unhook before; no colostomy bag or vital sign monitors. April gasped at first, but with a look from Cooper, she reached over and clicked a button to turn off the new tones that had erupted when he'd disconnected and she turned off his mattress. The only sounds associated with Cooper's body; the only monitoring of it, was to come from Cooper himself as he felt and experienced each movement, each gesture and each breath.

April and Derek still couldn't find any words. They simply smiled and laughed in nervous disbelief as Cooper moved his hands this way or that, like he was putting on a performance. He raised both hands up high and looked at them as though they couldn't possibly belong to him. He pulled them down into a bicep muscle pose for the two of them.

Cooper pushed his mom and Derek to either side of him and he looked at his legs, sizing them up. He felt them, running his fingers over his thighs and bending double over himself to feel his knees and shins and calves and feet. He touched each toe scientifically; Cooper was like a toddler picking at each digit curiously as if they were colorful keys on a plastic ring. He sat back up, one vertebrae at a time, while tracing his fingers up his legs until his hands were in his lap. He squeezed each leg. Cooper took a deep breath. Biting his lip and looking down at his feet, he wiggled first his right toes, then his left. His eyes were squinted and his brow was furrowed as though concentrating hard to make it happen. He rotated each ankle to the outside and then again to the inside. Cooper's lips spread open into a crooked, batty smile. His eyes shifted around trickily as if he was still taking in the scene around him; still convincing himself of this new reality. He was hungry for more experience.

Next, he looked at Derek and April as if to say, *should I?* He bent one knee, then the other very slowly. Cooper then planted his feet, which had been hovering an inch over the floor as he hung his legs off the side of the bed, onto the hardwood planks beneath him.

"Don't push yourself," Derek managed through baited breaths, but April was too overcome with crying to speak.

"I'm fine," Cooper whispered in focused concentration. He pushed the palms of his hands into his mattress on either side of himself and pursed his lips. Then, cautiously, he raised his body away from the bed and into a standing position.

"Cooper . . . how . . . but—" April began.

Cooper jumped on his legs, landing hard and flat-footed. He shifted his weight back and forth on his feet, the way he'd seen Matt Hill do on the pitcher's mound in the Wonder Kid dream. He bent both legs down so that he was squatting, and then he stood back up. Cooper spun around in the air to face his folks. There were no more tears; he grinned broadly down at them. His heart was beating quickly and he pushed his hand against his chest to feel it thumping within him. He absorbed every sensation. Cooper was so tuned into his body that he could almost feel his own blood flowing . . . buzzing through his veins and arteries. Suddenly, a light breeze brushed his face and Cooper inhaled the clean, night air that had come in through his open bedroom window. The mini-gust left the baseball-decorated curtains billowing in the air. He expanded his lungs to their full capacity, pushing out his stomach and feeling the cool breath fill him up like a human balloon. Cooper felt huge. He looked past April and Derek in a trancelike state toward the window.

"Oh," Cooper said in a new awe of the outdoors.

Then, as if the thought had just occurred to him, he said in an obsessed voice to his mom, "Wait! I gotta go!"

"You what?" she asked.

"Ha! I gotta go," he scoffed. With that he turned his back to them and started walking from the room. The steps began small as he crossed his room into the hallway. April and Derek both rose quickly to their feet. April began to step toward her son, but her husband held her back. Cooper held his hands out to the sides with fingers spread in a tiny tiptoe measure that made him look like a spy from old cartoons. Then, he began to take larger strides and eventually, halfway down the hall—his hands fell to his sides and swung normally while he relaxed his shoulders. He practically marched the rest of the way.

"Go where? What is going on?" Derek said to his wife.

"I don't even know *who* is going!" she exclaimed. "Follow," she indicated invitingly.

The two proceeded to shuffle out of the room after Cooper.

The bathroom door closed down the hallway. April and Derek looked at one another laughingly. They tried not to listen, but couldn't help overhearing a trickling sound, then a pause followed by a flush and water running in the sink. Next came the metal clunk stop of the faucet being turned off and the squeak of the hanging towel ring. After the awkward moment, Cooper flung the bathroom door open and stood in the doorway with his hands proudly planted on his hips. Silhouetted against the soft yellow light of the room behind him, Cooper looked like the profile of a hero.

"Yeah!" he shouted out spontaneously while he punched his fists into the air! "Yes! I did it!"

April and Derek broke into nervous, exhilarated laughter.

Cooper turned from the bathroom to go to other parts of the house. His pace had picked up to an easy jog across the house all the way to the front door, which he thrust open with twelve plus compounded years of pent up strength. Every door he threw open seemed to make him stand a little prouder and a little stronger. The front door slammed against the wall behind it just as the bathroom door before had done against the bathroom wall.

"Cooper?" asked Derek as he entered the living room with April right behind.

Cooper didn't turn around. Instead, he stepped out onto the porch and began to casually stroll all the way down his wheelchair ramp and the driveway until he reached the sidewalk. He beamed back at the two once more, then turned down the street and broke into an all-out sprint.

"Cooper!" called April in a frantic voice. "Cooper, it's the middle of the night! Cooper, come back!"

Cooper ran on, though. He was tired of listening.

"I'll get the van," said Derek and the two shuffled quickly to the garage.

Meanwhile, Cooper ran as fully as a body possibly could. Each step was like a leap and he swung his arms big and high. He pounded the pavement in a quick cadence and felt the night air rushing against his face and whistling past his ears. Cooper felt his heart begin to pound heavily and his lungs ache for deeper breaths. He kept going. He made it to the end of the block and ran right into the street. Nobody was out at this hour. He crossed without even pausing to look for traffic and he ran on. One house had a sprinkler out to water a lawn at night. Cooper ran right through it and circled back to do it again one more time, then two more times. He saw the headlights of the family van coming toward him, so he turned around and ran full out in the other direction back toward his house.

"Hey Mom! Hey Derek!" he shouted to them like a friendly neighbor as he passed the van.

"COOP!" scolded April.

The van turned around in a driveway and was caught back up to Cooper just as he made it to the house next to his own. Derek and April pulled into their driveway while Cooper plopped down breathlessly at last in his own front yard. His throat grew tight with thick breaths and a throbbing pulse. He spread his arms and legs as though he were making a snow angel. He stared up at the sky, panting away his vigorous run.

April was out of the van before it had even stopped and she ran to Cooper's side.

"Cooper, don't you *ever* do that again? Ever, ever, ever, EVER! I was worried sick!" she said.

"Cooper, are you okay?" said Derek running to join them.

"You're kidding, right?" said Cooper. "Never better!" Cooper jumped to his feet again.

"Don't you go running off again," April started in.

"I'm not!" Cooper said as he threw his arms around the necks of both Derek and his mom and squeezed them tightly with all the power he could muster. Finally, some of the tension in them softened.

"Come lay down," he offered. "The ground is nice." Cooper led them like a child to a sandcastle.

"But—" April objected. Cooper had already lain down. Derek plopped down on his butt beside his step son.

"Well, we need to call the doctor," she pled.

"It can wait, honey," said Derek. "Come sit with your husband and son."

April smiled good-naturedly down at them; clearly she wasn't going to win this argument. She sat at Cooper's other side. He held out a hand to each of them and the three lay linked.

"I'm calling when we go in, though," she said.

"Okay," Cooper shrugged lightly with cordial satisfaction. He listened to the night air sweep through desert bushes like maracas; a serenade to their midnight miracle. There was no sleep for any of them despite the aged hour. They lay in the yard until the dark sky melted into purples, then pinks, and finally a majestic, fiery pool of oranges and yellows. A hopeful sun was rising and birds were singing and Cooper simply concentrated on absorbing every sensation of the dawn into every inch of his being.

Chapter 14

Living the Dream

After what seemed like hundreds of phone calls to Aunt May and Uncle Harry, other relatives, friends, neighbors and everybody who ever knew or even heard of Cooper, April or Derek, there was a solid month of media frenzy. Newspapers, radio stations, local television and medical magazines all wanted to put their own little angle on the miracle boy. Sports organizations, Special Olympics and schools all wanted to hear what he had to say and every local feel-good group was asking for Cooper Ridge, the miracle boy; Cooper Ridge, The Wonder Kid . . . to be present at some function or other.

There were doctor's appointments, of course—and tests.

"It makes no sense, Mr. and Mrs. Lowell," one doctor said. "He shouldn't be moving at all. Even if he could, it still doesn't figure that he should know how to do the things he can do. These are learned actions, not instincts. One simply does not lie still for eight and a half years only to wake up running like a track star. I'm absolutely perplexed. Clearly he is strong and healthy and downright athletic, but I don't know why. Medicine doesn't always have the answers. If I were in your shoes, I'd simply be grateful for the blessings I'd been given and I'd appreciate every moment I had."

It was these moments for which Cooper lived. Not only was every single sensation one in which Cooper indulged—from sweating to itching to standing in a shower and letting the water run over himself; but every single action was one that he would use as an excuse to push his new bodily workings to their limits.

Every morning, Cooper woke to his alarm blaring and he would hop out of bed dancingly and plant his two feet against the cool, hard floor and wiggle his toes beneath him. He would do a loud, exaggerated stretch and he'd jump up and down in his bedroom as if he were a monkey on a big, room-sized trampoline.

Derek returned home from some errands one day with a package for Cooper.

"Got something for you!" he said with a casual grin as he tossed the box onto Cooper's bed.

Cooper tore into it like a starved man at a buffet.

"My own glove!" he called excitedly.

"Yeah, I was thinking—" began Derek.

"Thanks, Derek!" Cooper cut him off. "I'm gonna go show Nicholas!"

Cooper ran out of the room and house *with* his new baseball glove and *without* even noticing that Derek was holding a ball. The glove never left Cooper's side from that moment on. He used it, not just for baseball and sports, but also as an oven mitt and a hat and a shade over his face when he lay outside. Anything he could adapt to doing with that glove was done in such a matter.

That night, as with every night since the miracle, April and Derek tucked Cooper into bed, with his window cracked open. He waited awake until they were out of earshot. Then, Cooper would arise, go get cotton from the bathroom and tiptoe back to his room. He'd close his door behind him. Then, Cooper would shut his window and ball the cotton up tightly into his ears, pushing it deep inside so that there was no chance of it coming loose.

*   *   *

The dream he had each night was torture. For, there was no longer a different story every night . . . only the same one. Once Cooper would finally slip into an uneasy sleep, he'd relive the tense team try-out for the Washington Wonderboys. He slept with unwilling anticipation for the name that was bound to come. When at last the coach called out, "Danny Mills," Cooper tossed over through the fogginess and despite the aching blows against his warmed ears. The dream couldn't escape, though. It would then grow clear again and loop back for a replay. Throughout the night, Cooper would drift in and out of sleep trying to hold onto both the dream and his sanity at the same time. He was caught in limbo between the waking world and that of his imagined realities.

*   *   *

Every day, Cooper would run down the neighborhood street at a full sprint. Sometimes, he'd run right past Derek who carried around a baseball these days as if it were a wallet. It hung out in Derek's back pocket and he'd sigh a disappointed sigh as Cooper passed him by like an invisible presence.

When Cooper fell down on his runs, he would revel in the stinging pains brought by the sidewalk or road. He smiled through the cool cleansings that dissipated the burn in the scrape or cut; his mom had grown used to performing her new type of nursing duties and Cooper was proud of the bandages that were applied to the raw road rashes. While April would wish hopefully that this meant Cooper was in for the day, he'd simply brush himself off and start running once more.

*   *   *

But again, at night—after the window was shut and the cotton was pushed into his ears, the dream would return, keeping Cooper caught in limbo between the waking world and that of his imagined realities.

*   *   *

In the afternoon, after the local schools had let out for the day, Cooper would run to meet Nicholas at the park and watch his friend's team play. Cooper hadn't been able to try out for the team, but because his miraculous recovery had made him into something of a local hero, he was allowed a uniform of his own. He was the bat boy and he got to toss out every opening pitch for the whole local little league; he'd actually run between the different fields at the top of each hour tossing out the pitch for each of the four games that went on each hour on Saturday morning and a couple of hours on some weeknights. He was allowed to run the bases to open and close important games and he basked in the echo of his name being called in the stands by his friends and family and neighbors.

After the games were done each Saturday, while Derek sat with April in the bleachers with a hopeful look on his face and a baseball in his hand, an unnoticing Cooper would shout out, "I'm going over to Nicholas' house now! See you guys later!"

The two would smile but looked drained.

*   *   *

And, of course, at night—after the window was shut and the cotton was pushed into his ears, the dream would return, keeping Cooper caught in limbo between the waking world and that of his imagined realities.

*   *   *

In the evening, when families had retired to their own homes, Derek and April would attempt to enjoy a meal around the table with Cooper. Both would ask about his day and his plans with the team.

"You know," Derek began at one such meal. "Nobody is playing on the field this weekend after the games. And also, the fields won't be raked and chalked until Sunday. So, for all of Saturday night it's free."

"I have an idea!" Cooper said excitedly.

"Yes?" responded an equally excited Derek.

"Mom! How about I can take some of these ribs down to Nicholas' house? I love this sauce!" he exclaimed, completely ignoring Derek. Food was another new love of Cooper's.

"Um, I suppose," she sighed.

Cooper gathered up most of what was left on the table and put it onto a sheet of aluminum foil which he folded up and then headed for the door.

"See you in time for bed," he called back absently as the door shut behind him.

If he'd still been as keen on listening as he was when he was a quadriplegic, Cooper would have heard April say, "It's just all new to him, Derek. Maybe in another couple of weeks, he'll want to have a catch."

April reassured her husband with a gentle touch and affectionate eyes as he rolled the baseball, which he had pulled from out of his back pocket, around on the surface of the table.

*   *   *

Cooper was home in time for bed as he promised. After the window was shut and the cotton was pushed into his ears, the dream returned, keeping Cooper caught in limbo between the waking world and that of his imagined realities.

*   *   *

Spring melted into summer and summer burned its color into Cooper's flesh; now tanned and freckled with healthful youth—just as Danny Mills' had been in the The Wonder Kid dream. Each of Cooper's days was spent fully awake, frolicking in the pleasures of the world. Each of his nights was spent, with the window shut and cotton in his ears, fighting a dream that would constantly return and replay—a dream that was attempting to escape; the dream that kept Cooper caught in limbo between the waking world and that of his imagined realities.

Chapter 15

Washington and The Wonderboys

After another nearly sleepless night, Cooper was awoken not by his alarm clock, but the telephone.

"Hello?" April answered.

"Oh, hey sis," she continued after a pause.

"Oh you know it's all still just so hard to believe. Every day is a gift. But, time is flying so fast. I feel like Derek and I haven't even gotten to take part in this new life of his," she sighed heavily into the phone.

"May, I'm sorry. I didn't even ask why you called. I know while we've been dealing with this unexpected positive, you've been dealing with an unexpected negative. How's that boy doing?" Cooper heard his mom ask, and then there was a long pause during which April responded with the occasional *"Oh,"* or a genuinely concerned, *"I'm so sorry, sis,"* or, *"I just wish there was something I could do."*

Then, the tone of the conversation changed and—with excitement in her voice, Cooper's mom exclaimed, "That's a great idea! He'd love it. I'm sure!"

There was talk of dates and times and the travel voucher that Cooper had gotten at Christmas from Aunt May and Uncle Harry and—as the call came to a close before the inevitable *"love you"* and *"goodbye"* and the click of the phone in its carriage, Cooper had grown certain that the talk was about him.

"What was that all about?" he said groggily to his mom in the kitchen as he pretended to be just waking.

"Good morning, Sleepyhead! Well, I haven't had much chance to talk to you about this, Bud," April said as she poured cereal for her son and herself and the two sat at the kitchen counter.

"Or maybe," she went on, "I just didn't really think that there was a good time to bring it up. You've been having so much fun and I didn't want to rain on your joy. You're my boy. I want you to be happy."

April ruffled Cooper's hair and stroked his cheek like she used to do before they could hug. Cooper brushed her off, as a twelve-year-old boy often does to an affectionate mother.

"What, mom?" he muttered into his cereal spoon.

She smiled at him with a deep shrug of her shoulders. "Aunt May has been having a hard time in Washington."

"Why?"

"Well, you know how she works for the community recreation department, right?"

"Yeah."

"There are two sides of the department and she does physical therapy for both."

"You mean the regular teams and the Special Olympics side?"

"That's right. They have a wonderful little league team, there. You would have a great time watching them. *The Washington Wonderboys*," her words seemed to echo endlessly and loudly in his raw, aching eardrums.

Cooper nearly choked on his flakes as he coughed milk back into his bowl and it splashed into his nose.

"You okay?" asked April.

"Sorry. Yeah. Fine. Wrong tube," he gargled. "What about them? The team?" he questioned, trying to sound as casual as possible while he wiped up his face and pinched his nostrils with the napkin

"Well, apparently—and this is why I didn't really want to tell you because I thought it may bring you down—but, one of the boys on that team became paralyzed this year. Nobody knows why. He was the MVP last year . . . a very healthy, athletic young boy, same age as you. While you've been living this wonder of recoveries, that young boy has become a quadriplegic. He just woke up in the middle of the night and wasn't able to move."

Cooper stared at his mom with glossy eyes. His mind was racing. *It has to be a coincidence*, he thought. *It couldn't be The Washington Wonderboys from his dreams.*

"I know you're still getting used to . . . you know," she went on. "I just . . . well, your Aunt May and I . . . we were hoping that maybe you might be able to go visit her. She really needs to be around something good right now and also maybe you could meet this other boy. His situation is not very good, Coop. I don't mean it's bad because he's paralyzed. It's different from you, Bud. He doesn't have what you had . . . not the quality of life; maybe not even the length of life. It takes more than just good will to make it. It takes a lot of things that you took for granted and they didn't come cheap. I can't explain, really. You'll see for yourself."

"What? I'm going? But, you didn't even ask me!" he whined.

"Why are you so upset? I thought you'd understand, Cooper. And you'll get to visit with your aunt and uncle. Why would this *not* be something you'd want to do?"

"I just don't want to!" he exclaimed.

"Cooper, you're going," she firmly said as she cleared away the dishes hastily in apparent anger. His spoon was still hovering over the bowl when the bowl was snapped from beneath it. Then his mom snatched the spoon out of his hand, too, as she went on.

"I can't believe after everything you have been given, you can't so much as share your *time*. Guess I shouldn't be surprised since you haven't shared it with Derek or I, either. Believe me, son. It is the least you can do for your aunt. But, who is she, anyway, besides the person who kept you *ALIVE* for eight years?!" April was now shouting.

Cooper stared back at her, still glazed over. His mother had never scolded him before; ever. He was in shock.

"Cooper, I don't know who you are these days," she went on angrily. You disappoint me," she shook her head.

"It's just that . . . I . . . I mean—" but Cooper couldn't come up with a good reason as to why he shouldn't go see Aunt May and Uncle Harry. Much less could he come up with some sort of acceptable excuse to get out of meeting the boy he *hoped* he didn't already know; the boy whose name he refused to ask because he was afraid to hear it.

Besides, his mom wasn't going to hear any argument over the matter. Cooper could never remember her being so upset that she actually raised her voice and then, to use the word *disappointed!* He felt like he'd fallen off the top of the world at that moment and he was actually looking forward to the trip just so that he'd be able to get out of the house that had grown hostile and hurtful with the words exchanged between him and his mother.

So it was that one week later, young Cooper found himself, his new glove, and a bag of cotton balls on an airplane headed north with a suitcase full of clothes beneath him in the belly of the plane. He slept the whole trip up, with his baseball glove as a pillow and cotton in his ears, of course.

"It helps keep my ears from popping," he'd told the flight attendant who looked at him strangely when he stuffed the balled up fluff deep into his ear canals.

When he'd gotten off the plane, Aunt May and Uncle Harry were waiting excitedly at the gate. He spotted them searching the crowd of exiting passengers to see their nephew's face. They scanned right past him twice each! Finally, when he made eye-contact with his uncle, he grinned at him and mouthed, "Hi!" His uncle's jaw dropped and he squeezed May's shoulder and pointed. Immediately, Aunt May's hands went to her mouth and she shook her head in disbelief. Cooper could see the wells of tears sparkling in her warm eyes.

"Oh, Cooper!" she gushed as he joined their outstretched arms. "I never dreamed you were so tall," she said laughingly.

"You look great, guy!" said his uncle. His cheeks appled up with an unstoppable, ear-to-ear smile.

Cooper felt in many ways that he was reliving his first movements again all day long. Aunt May and Uncle Harry kept staring and had painted on smiles that never seemed to wear down. Occasionally, his aunt would break into uncontrollable fits of giggles—something Cooper never recalled seeing from her in the past. His uncle, big teddy bear that he was, kept wrapping Cooper up in an unexpected and very strong, tight squeeze.

The three spent that first day and night catching up, getting Cooper set up in the guest room and going out to eat. Uncle Harry laughed heartily when his nephew ordered a *steak* at the restaurant.

In the days following his arrival, Cooper began to think that he'd escape having to discover the inevitable reality of why he was here; meeting the Washington Wonderboys and the boy who was paralyzed. Instead, the time was spent seeing local attractions, shopping for state souvenirs to bring back to his mom, Derek and Nicholas and visiting construction sites for which his uncle was the foreman.

The night before Cooper's departure, though, Uncle Harry popped in on Cooper in the guest room.

"Got something for you, guy!" he grinned while he tossed a baseball cap at Cooper. Cooper turned it around and saw the logo that was an unmistakable match with one he'd seen in his dreams. It was a Washington Wonderboys cap, with Cooper's own name added above the logo.

"Why don't you grab that glove you're always toting around and come with me!" said his uncle.

"I'll need my glove?"

"Well, it's a baseball field! Can't think of a better place for it."

The drive to the practice field was filled with the stats and histories that Uncle Harry had learned about the local championship team.

"They're still playing?" Cooper asked.

"Well, they didn't make the championship this year, but they've still got a couple of local games left."

When the two arrived, the team was out on the pitch, in the midst of a practice game against themselves. Cooper looked out to the mound and inhaled an involuntary gasp.

It was Matt Hill.

"He's really good," Cooper noted after watching Matt wing in a few pitches. The ball seemed to whiz by faster than he could remember . . . *if* he could remember.

"They're all good," said Uncle Harry. "They're all great, actually. But, they lost the game in their hearts, this year. They just weren't in it."

"Harry!" called an older man coming to the fence where Cooper stood with his uncle. It was the coach; another face Cooper immediately recognized. In his head, worlds he never truly thought connected began to collide.

"Glad you could make it down!" he exclaimed. "This must be the boy, then?"

"Yep, my nephew, Cooper Ridge. Miracle. He's *our* Wonder Kid." Both Cooper and the coach seemed to flinch simultaneously at this statement. "Coop, you can call this man *Coach,*" finished Uncle Harry.

"Hey . . . *Coach,*" he stuttered awkwardly.

"What are you doing on that side? You brought your glove, right? Come on over. Play a bit with us!" he responded cheerfully.

"You can use this!" he added with a broad grin while he brandished a baseball bearing the stamped symbol of the Little League World Championship Game. "It's yours after today if you want it."

Cooper looked to his uncle for permission, almost hoping that it wouldn't come, but he nodded with proud approval. Cooper donned his glove and went around the fence to join the Washington Wonderboys. Part of him kept waiting for the world around him to grow blurry. It never did. As unbelievable as it seemed, this was real.

"Jump in at shortstop, why don't you?" directed Coach.

"Yes, sir," Cooper said.

The boys on the team all had stopped to watch Cooper walk across their field. He could hear their whispers. He could feel their eyes on his legs; watching him walk. As he was passing Matt, his heart began to race.

"Hey, you that kid that couldn't move last year?" asked the pitcher while he was still within earshot.

"That's me," said Cooper. "I was paralyzed." The words sounded stupid and obvious to him.

"Cool," he said. "I mean, cool *now*," He corrected himself.

"Thanks."

"You should come by after practice," Matt offered.

"Um . . . um . . . I guess," Cooper was caught off guard by the invitation. "I have to make sure it's okay with my aunt and uncle."

"Cool. You do that. Now, get out there," said Matt with a nod toward the empty shortstop position. Cooper remembered a different Matt from his dream of the season's tryouts; a boy who was confident and fun and playful. This young man came across as strong and determined and—Cooper hated the thought—but, a little bit bitter, too.

They played for a couple of hours. In the outfield, Cooper didn't let a ball by. There seemed to be in him, some inherent knowledge of the skills necessary to working that position. Even though the baseball was constantly punching against the leather of his glove, though, Cooper felt that he didn't belong here.

When it was his turn to bat, he swung and missed against Matt's first two pitches. Then, on the third, he circled that bat down hard, strong and straight, ending with a resounding smack against the wood. The ball flew farther and farther out, still too high to be caught by the

Wonderboys in deep field. Finally, a slow, arcing descent culminated in the ringing bell-like clangs of the ball against the metal bleachers outside of the fence. It was a homerun.

Cooper ran the bases to the cheers of the Washington Wonderboys and felt—for a moment—full of joy. It may only have been a scrimmage, but he had given his all and done his best. Then, as he felt Matt's eyes burning holes into his running legs, the feeling of elation faded. Cooper knew that he didn't belong here.

When all was said and done, Cooper gathered his glove and met his proud looking uncle outside the fence. Much to his dismay, Uncle Harry had already met Mr. and Mrs. Hill and agreed to let Cooper visit them for dinner.

The ride to the Hill house was tense. Cooper didn't know what to say to any of these people and Matt had plenty to ask of Cooper.

"So, what did you do the day before you started moving again?" he questioned.

"Nothing, really. I went out with my step-dad," Cooper said.

"What did you eat?"

"I don't really remember. I think I had some soup. The rest was nothing different than usual."

"With your breathing tube?"

"I didn't have breathing tubes. I have a special thing—kind of like a pacemaker—but, for my diaphragm instead of my heart. It makes . . . I mean . . . *made* me breathe."

"Oh. Well, what else did you have? What other stuff to help you out? Did you have a nurse or . . ."

"Matt, give the young man a rest," Mrs. Hill finally chimed in.

Matt said he was sorry, but still looked at Cooper in a way that Cooper could only interpret as resentful. His own mouth turned upward meekly before he looked outside the car window. Finally, they were pulling into the family drive. It was a farm. Something seemed familiar. The car stopped in front of a red barn. On the side of the barn, a batter's box had been chalked. It was partly erased from rain and wind, but the pasty, yellow residue that remained was clear enough to make out as something that had obviously been drawn in the same place time and again over the course of many months or even years.

"Hey," said Cooper getting out of the car. "Isn't this house . . . I mean," he stopped himself. "This is where *you* live?"

"Yeah," said Matt.

"*Just* you guys?" Cooper asked.

"Now. My friend and his dad used to rent the barn. The whole upper floor of it has been converted to a sort of living quarters."

"They lived in the barn?"

"Not always," he said casually. "My dad and his dad were friends their whole lives. When my friend's mom got real sick with cancer, they spent everything they had on trying to make her better. But, she died and they had nothing left, so they came to live here."

"Where are they now?" Cooper questioned with concern.

Matt sized him up for a minute before answering. "Danny's in a facility."

Cooper had his confirmation. He hated the sound of the name that he had once yearned to hear and that now tortured him every night while he slept.

"His dad, Mr. Mills, he has to work a lot to afford the place that takes care of my friend and we told him he could stay here, but he didn't want to be any trouble," Matt continued. "So, he's got some tiny little place in town for just himself. It's closer to Danny, so he can walk to see him. His car ain't too reliable or anything."

"Sorry," said Cooper.

"Well," interrupted Matt's dad with a change of subject. "Let's get in and feed you boys after you worked so hard out there on that field!"

Dinner was uncomfortable for Cooper. Although the Hill family was certainly hospitable and the conversation was warm, he couldn't help but feel he was on display the whole time. When his aunt arrived to bring him back to the house, he was relieved.

"Oh wait!" interjected Mrs. Hill as Aunt May and Cooper were headed out. "I have some things for Danny. You'll be seeing him tomorrow, right, May?"

"Yes. I'm bringing Cooper," she responded. Cooper did a double take at these words because his aunt hadn't told him yet about the impending visit and he'd still been hoping that it had been forgotten in the itinerary.

"Well, come back in for just a quick second. I have to bag up the clothes."

Cooper and his aunt returned to the tense household once more and followed Mrs. Hill to a back bedroom where she had clothing lain out that had clearly been just washed and folded. "I know it's not much," she began as she stuffed the clothes into a bag. Cooper bit his lip shamefully as he noted the items; the jeans with beige stitching, a striped polo t-shirt and there—he swallowed—were the signature white leather tennis shoes. "It's all I could get from the church in his size. Tell him that we promise to bring some more . . . you know . . . modern clothes just as soon as we get paid. I know these aren't exactly in."

"Oh, honey. You just don't know that boy," said Aunt May. "He is so grateful for everything you send. It doesn't matter to him how it looks."

Cooper noticed moisture glistening off the fake-smiling eyes of Mrs. Hill.

"I'm sorry," she said. "I can't believe I still get like this," She fanned her hand at her eyes as if batting away the tears. "Matt, too. He says that all Danny had in life was his dad and his baseball and now," her voice broke. "Now, he has neither."

"It's okay. It's okay," Aunt May said with a hug to Mrs. Hill.

"And Cooper," continued Matt's mom as she broke from Aunt May's hug, wiped away tears and took a strengthening breath while she turned to face him, "I hope you will forgive our curiosity with you. Especially Matt's. We just know that there's an answer inside of you somewhere and we all love Danny Mills so very much that we want to help find it. The whole town loves him, in fact. He's The Wonder Kid, after all. Danny Mills, The Wonder Kid."

"It's okay," said Cooper. Not a question remained as to who the boy was. Every piece of the puzzle was nearly in place and Cooper would have to look at the mirror of his own soul in the morning when he met the real Wonder Kid.

*   *   *

The night was yet another restless one for Cooper. The dream was the usual repetitive torture and in between the blurring out of the night vision, his own guilty thoughts played at tap dancing around in his head.

Chapter 16

The Real Danny Mills

In the morning, Cooper packed his belongings and the gifts for his mom, Derek and Nicholas. He shoved a handful of cotton balls into his pockets before putting the remainder of the bag into his carry-on suitcase, along with his glove. Then, after breakfast, he waited for his aunt to be ready for work.

When they arrived at the rehabilitation facility, Cooper was shocked at the appearance of the place. It was clean, but aside from that, it looked more like a dungeon than the types of places he had been in when he was in the early stages of his paralysis. The rooms were a gray-white with barren walls and a small, singular, square window each.

"Alright, Coop," began his aunt while she pulled out a chart. "You're really going to like this boy. Just talk to him. Talk to him about baseball. He'll love that. Now, let me take a look here. It's hard to believe it's been so long. He's been paralyzed since," she paused as she scanned the chart. "Hmmm . . . . wow. How ironic. I guess I never thought about the date before. He stopped moving on the same day that you began. I think I'd not mention that to him. Okay? In fact, we still don't have any answers for him. Just like you woke up moving in the middle of the night, he woke up not being able to. Could you just sort of hang out like he's fine. You remember what it's like needing that, right?"

Cooper nodded respectfully to his aunt.

"It means a lot to me that you're visiting Danny."

"Sure," said Cooper.

He peeked into the room with the boy from his dreams. Danny's hair was combed greasily to one side. Tubes were hooked up to him and his skin was practically a transparent blue, with yellows and purples at the entrance points of all of the various tubes, needles and other assistants. Cooper felt sorry for the once Wonder Kid. When he opened the door, a scent was in the air that made him swallow back a gag reflex unwillingly.

"It's my leg," said Danny in an off-handed tone. Cooper snapped to him. He didn't realize that the boy had noticed him coming in.

"What?"

"The smell. It catches everyone off-guard the first time they come in. It's my leg. It's rotting. The doctors say they'll probably have to take it soon. They do their best here. Especially nurse May. But, she's only here once a week. I just don't get enough movement."

"May is my aunt. So, you might lose your leg?"

"They say."

"Don't you have a special mattress so that there aren't pressure spots?"

"Naw. They don't have that fancy stuff here! Wouldn't be bad if I could get on the equipment more, but a lot of patients share it and it's more important to let people who could regain movement use it."

"Is that what they told you?"

"No. It's just my own thought. I'm on a waiting list for some really great things, though and—as for the leg—well, they have some pretty awesome new prosthetics these days, too, if I ever actually want one. It wouldn't work, anyway, though; just for my studly good looks," Danny finished with an actual smile at his own joke.

Cooper opened his mouth to say something in return, but no words seemed right.

"So, that's your aunt?" Danny continued to break the momentary silence. "Then you must be that Cooper kid, huh," Danny's voice was quiet and breathy and it seemed a labor for him to talk at all, but his tone was still upbeat.

"I guess."

"Sit down," he smiled.

Cooper couldn't believe how cordial and kind Danny Mills was. He put Coop immediately at ease and in no time he noticed neither the smell, nor the whispering of the machines, nor the way his new friend couldn't move. After small talk about his aunt, the people Cooper had met in the town and the weather, the conversation eventually turned to the subject he had expected would be necessary to ease the comfort level; baseball.

"I had this game-winning catch last year—" Danny began.

"I know," Cooper couldn't help but say.

"You do?"

"Um . . . it was national, so I read about it. My step dad and I, we follow all the baseball news . . . even little league," Cooper covered.

"Man, it was cool," Danny said. "It was like the whole world stopped while that fly was falling down on me and I reached as far as I could and leapt up as high as I could and that ball smacked against my glove so hard—"

"That it stung all the way down your body to your toes until they crumpled beneath you back on the ground," finished Cooper.

"Yeah. Yeah, that's exactly it!" nodded Danny in excited agreement. "Nobody has ever described it better."

"I can imagine," said Cooper. "Do you miss it?" he asked as if he honestly wished Danny would say, *no*.

"Of course I miss it. But, I'm glad I have it to miss," said the Mills boy unexpectedly.

"What do you mean?"

"Well, it means it happened. I gave my all and did my best. Can you imagine never being able to play ball?"

"Yes. I can," said Cooper pointedly.

"Oh. Sorry. That's right. I guess you can. See, though? You're fine now. There's hope for me."

"To make the team again?"

"Oh, I don't care about that," Danny sputtered.

"You don't?"

"Well, it'd be nice to be The Wonder Kid, again, but mostly I just want to be an ordinary kid, you know?" he said somewhat sadly.

"Yeah. Yeah, actually, I know exactly what you mean."

"Do you want to know what I really miss most?" he questioned Cooper.

"What?"

"Just playing around with my dad—no championships, no crowds—just having him pitch to me. Shoot! Even just having a catch. That was the best part," Danny was lost in reminiscence for a moment. Then, he snapped himself back into the conversation.

"Your step dad throw a few with you?"

"Um . . ." began Cooper. "No. No he hasn't. We haven't"

"Really?"

"Well, not yet."

"Hmm. Too bad. You're missing out," Danny said with glazed over eyes as his mind seemed to wander back to the happy memory once again.

He was missing out, thought Cooper? How could Danny Mills lie there motionless, unable to breathe on his own, maybe about to lose his leg completely and say that Cooper was the one who was missing out?

The personal conversation melted away once more into talk of baseball players and stats. They discussed the Arizona Diamondbacks and the Seattle Mariners and who would take the series and in how many games if the two unlikely champions were to face one another. They talked about how the Washington Wonderboys didn't make it that year to the little league championship, but that they were still finishing out their season and they'd have a good chance next year. Danny's best pal Matt would be going as a spectator to the championship, though, and he promised to take lots of pictures for Danny.

The morning talk between the two boys lost in the limbo between crippled and incredible was long and pleasant. Time ticked away to mid-day. Cooper forgot his guilt for a moment, trying to convince himself that Danny was better at being laid up than Cooper ever was. It didn't take much to remind Cooper of his selfishness, though.

"Hey, there's my son!" said a man coming into the room.

"Dad!" Danny called. He didn't need to say it. Cooper immediately recognized the elder Mills from his dreams. He looked so much more tired now, though; his hair was grayer and his skin was lighter and he'd lost some weight. Mr. Mills still had the same blue eyes, though—despite now lacking the sparkle that Cooper had noticed in them in the dream he stole.

Danny smiled up at his dad and had so much life in his face that—for an instant—Cooper could imagine him moving again. Then, almost as though Danny himself had been feeling the same thing, the smile unwillingly disappeared off of his face. He simply couldn't return love to his dad the way he wanted. No matter how you try, you can't hug with a smile. He put that smile back, though in at least a feeble attempt.

"I was just stopping by," said his dad pretending not to notice Danny's mood change. "I had some time between jobs. But, it looks like you've got company, already," finished Mr. Mills while he ruffled his son's hair the same way Cooper had witnessed in the championship dream nearly a year ago. He forced a broad grin even though his eyes had heavy bags and his hair was overdue for a cut.

"Yeah, Dad. This is Cooper Ridge," Danny indicated with a nod.

"Oh! Nurse May's nephew, right?" he asked with an offered hand.

"That's right," Cooper answered with a shake.

"We've heard about you, alright!" he exclaimed. "Haven't we, son?" he added to Danny. "You give us hope. You are the miracle. Not that we need one, right Danny? You'll always be The Wonder Kid to me."

Danny widened his smile for his Dad and it didn't look fake this time. Maybe he could learn to hug without touching. Mr. Mills spoke quickly and shakily as if choking back tears. He simultaneously glowed with pride and grayed with heartbreak while looking down at his son on the bed. Cooper sensed an emotional moment coming on for which he did not want to be present.

"I should go," he said. "I have a plane to catch. It was nice meeting both of you. You're gonna be okay, Danny Mills," Cooper added.

"I hope so," said Danny, his eyes turned toward Coop.

"I know so," Cooper returned after a pause with a deep, knowing nod.

"Have a good trip," Mr. Mills offered.

Danny nodded to Cooper, but the joy in his face from the moments of sharing memories had long faded away. Mr. Mills shook his hand again and Cooper noticed how those roughened fingers trembled ever so slightly while his eyes shone with clear moisture and he nodded his close-lipped smile to Cooper.

"Well, um . . . bye," Cooper finished awkwardly. He exited and peeked back through the window of the room. Almost instantaneously as the door shut behind him, Mr. Mills collapsed into sobs on his son's chest. He reached his arms up to stroke his son's cheeks.

"Dad, don't," Danny cried with him. "It's okay, Dad. Don't make me cry. It's hard to breathe when I do," he choked out. Cooper stared at the breathing tube attached to Danny's neck and the tubes and wires and bags and drips going in and out of his body.

"I'm so sorry I can't afford to bring you home yet, son. I promise it will be soon. The second I've got enough to get somebody to take care of you, even if I have to work a third job. I miss having you around, Danny. I promise you'll come home."

"Thanks, Coop," came Aunt May's softer-than-usual voice from behind him. He quickly turned around. "Did you boys have a good conversation?"

"It was fine," said Cooper plainly, but his mind was racing.

"Good. It means a lot to me that you visited. We really need to get you to the airport, though. Your Uncle is doing a double check to make sure we've got everything in the car."

"Hey, I got her all loaded up down there," said Uncle Harry exiting the elevator as if on cue. "You sure pack a lot for a week, Bud! You have a nice visit?"

"It was great," he replied with a stern expression.

Chapter 17

The Wake-Up Call

Aunt May and Uncle Harry took Cooper to the airport and saw him through all the way to the gate where they left him with kisses and roughed up hair. He waved back to them tiredly as he moved out of sight and onto his plane. It had been a trying day and he planned to sleep the whole way home to Arizona.

Cooper requested a blanket and pillow from the flight attendant. He reached into his pocket and pulled out two cotton balls that he had stuffed into his jeans that morning. He balled up the cotton tightly and put it into his ears. Then he blocked out the visit with the real Danny Mills, The Wonder Kid by shutting his heavy eyes.

* * *

He was on the bench again on that cold, Washington morning, listening to coach read off the roster.

"Matt Hill, Pitcher!" said the coach.

Next, Coach read off the name of the catcher, 1st base, 2nd base, 3rd base . . .

"And for shortstop, we have a new starter this year," he began. "Danny Mills, come on over!" he called to Cooper.

The real Cooper Ridge flinched in his sleep. His ears burned and his dream blurred.

"And for shortstop, we have a new starter this year," he began. "Danny Mills, come on over!" he called to Cooper.

Cooper turned again and huffed away the dream's escape attempt. Clarity returned to his sleep-induced imagining.

"Danny Mills, come on over!" Coach called. The dream faded in, then out, then refocused again.

"Danny Mills, come on over!" the loop continued.

"Danny Mills. Danny Mills. Danny Mills. Danny Mills. Danny Mills. Danny Mills," the voice rang again and again and again in his head. There was no longer any blurriness between the replays of the dream in his mind. Coach, then coach's face, then coach's mouth seemed to grow larger and more and more into focus. The dream was at war, trying to bomb its way out.

"Danny Mills. Danny Mills," the nightmare name came in a nonstop stream of calls that pounded against his throbbing ears like a hammer with each repetition.

"Danny Mills, DANNY MILLS, DANNY MILLS!" the voice shouted and grew deeper and louder and pushed so hard against his ears that Cooper felt sure his head was about to explode; pushed apart from within.

"DANNY MILLS!" the voice shrilly screamed at last.

"STOP IT!" hollered a fully awake Cooper. People all around the plane were staring.

*   *   *

"Can I help you, honey," said a flight attendant in a calming, discreet whisper. "You were tossing around like crazy."

"Sorry," said a breathless Cooper. "Just a bad dream," he added as he pulled out the cotton balls from his ears. Clearly he wouldn't be sleeping on this trip.

"Oh. Cotton in the ears. A lot of people get earaches on planes, honey. I understand," she said. "You just let us know if you need anything. I'm right down the aisle." She squeezed Cooper's arm lovingly and looked kindly down at him. Cooper relaxed his panting breath as he took in the flight attendant's kindness.

She began to walk away, but a shaken Cooper called her back.

"Just one thing," he said.

"What is it, dear?" she asked turning back toward him.

"Will it still be light when we land?"

"Oh yes. Plenty of daylight left, honey," she assured him with that gentle smile.

"Good," he said. "I have something I have to do. Thank you, ma'am."

"Sure thing," she said sweetly.

Cooper stared out the window for the rest of the flight. Unwilling tears filled the bottoms of his eyes, but he stubbornly blinked them away as he took a deep, calming breath.

His plane landed while the sun still shone in the Arizona sky. No sky in the world compared to a desert sunset. Derek and his mom greeted him at the gate with hugs.

"We missed you," April gushed. "How was your trip?"

"Tiring," he yawned.

"Didn't you sleep on the plane?" she questioned.

"Couldn't," replied Cooper.

"I know what you mean," Derek interjected. "I can never sleep on planes. My ears pop like crazy. Hurts."

"Tell me about it," said Cooper.

The three drove home and Cooper told them all about his Aunt and Uncle's new place and the Washington Wonderboys.

"May told me that you talked to that poor boy, Danny Miller, too," April said.

"Mills. Danny Mills," Cooper corrected her.

"Nice boy?" she asked.

"The best."

"And how's he doing?"

"He, uh . . ." Cooper stopped. He didn't know what to say.

"Not so good, huh? That must have been hard."

"Yeah. Everybody seems to think I have the answer."

"Well, that's a lot of pressure, Bud."

"It's okay, though. Maybe I *can* help."

"Sure you can," chimed in Derek. "You just do what you think is best."

"Yeah. What I think is best," Cooper finished, mostly to himself.

The casual catch-up conversation ended then as Cooper's mind drifted to his evening plans.

Chapter 18

Having a Catch

When they got home, Cooper took his things to his room and he began to unpack. His bedroom was a little cluttered. He'd have to take care of that. There was something else he had to do first. He pulled his glove out from his carry-on suitcase and put it on, pounding it with his fist. It was still slightly dusty from the Washington field. He took out the ball from the Wonderboys that Coach had let him take and he dropped it to himself a couple of times. He loved the sound of the ball as it echoed within his leather mitt. Then, he headed to the kitchen.

"Derek?" Cooper timidly began when he got to the kitchen and saw his mom and step dad at the counter sharing a glass of iced tea.

"What's up, Coop?" he asked casually.

"Well, I was wondering if maybe you'd like to have a catch?"

"Really?"

"Yeah. I got this new ball and Mom, you can come, too."

"We'd love to!" exclaimed April, barely able to contain herself. Meanwhile, Derek had already left the room and was returning with the gloves for April and himself.

The summer air was calm and the world seemed to stand still, keeping the sun hanging like an ornament in the sky even longer than it should have. It was almost as though the day stretched on for just Cooper and his family while they shared a seasonal pastime. He, his mom and Derek laughed and talked and tossed the ball between one another. Derek worked Cooper at fielding the ball high, low and to each side. Cooper whipped the stitched sphere to his mom with all of his might and she pretended the catch stung.

When they finally went in, (only after the sun had long gone, the dusk had faded and the fluorescent streetlights began to blink on), it was with sore shoulders and dry throats that were to be quenched with lemonade. The three enjoyed burgers done on the grill and topped with lettuce and tomato. Cooper ate slowly, savoring every bite. Dinner conversation was buzzing with the reliving of tales from the summer. It was the perfect end to the perfect day in the perfect dream.

Later that night, Cooper sat on the edge of his bed holding his baseball glove. It was worn from months of constant use. He felt the soft leather by running his fingers over each curve of the digits; he closed his eyes and took in every worn spot, every stitch, every smooth surface, and every inch that had gone bald straight down to the linen-like stubble left behind when the oiled, light brown surface had served its time. He had given his best with this glove—and having finally had a catch with Derek and his mom; it had given him something in return.

At the touch of his glove, Cooper mourned. He mourned the loss of the person he once was. Without the use of most of his body, he never had a problem sharing his heart. He had been grateful for the things that he *did* have. With his arms and legs, though, he had had grown selfish and allowed others to suffer for his gifts. And what about his mom and Derek? All they wanted when he received his blessing of movement was to enjoy it with him. All he could think to do was to be away from the home and people that had held him safely for so long . . . keeping his new accomplishments—his new *life* to himself.

Cooper also mourned the possibility that the dreams would never return again; the dreams that gave him those gifts. Last, he mourned the person he could have been if he'd remembered to use that most *important* part of himself when he'd gained the use of *every* part. *No more,* he thought. *I know what matters, now. I know what's best. I just hope it's not too late.*

Cooper rose from his bed with the glove and he walked over to his top dresser drawer. He put his glove in the drawer, and then closed it. Cooper took the bag of cotton balls out of his carry-on and brought them to the bathroom. When he returned to his room, he picked up all of his things from the floor and straightened everything to make a clear path and neatly kept area. In his closet, his chair was folded up with his bat-boy uniform lying across the top of it. Cooper hung up the uniform, trying not to focus on his wheelchair and then he took from his closet the signed bat and his old, loose yo-yo. Next, he turned off the closet's light and shut its door.

There's just one thing left to do, thought Cooper as he looked at his bedroom window. Determined to follow-through, he crossed the room. He balanced the bat against his window ledge and put the yo-yo upon the nightstand beneath his lamp. Cooper turned the lock on the window and opened it wide. A gust of fresh, Arizona air rushed the room and steeled him in his decision. The tassel-like ends of some of the pennants on his walls fluttered lightly.

Cooper propped his pillows and changed into a newly cleaned pair of pajamas. He turned his alarm off as he had no desire to wake to face the next day. He turned on his pressure changing mattress that had been silenced months ago. The sound of the tiny motor and whispering of air flow began immediately. It was a resigned sound. When his mom and Derek came in to say goodnight, Cooper pulled his mom to him in a bear hug and squeezed with all his might.

"My goodness, Coop!" April laughed. "What did I do to deserve this?"

"Nothing," he said while still holding onto his mom tightly. "Just wanted to give you a good hug."

"Did you turn on your mattress? What's that all about?"

"Just thought it might help me sleep after that plane ride. It was so uncomfortable."

"Okay, Bud."

"G'night, Coop," Derek added to the moment with a tight squeeze to Cooper's arm. Cooper let the squeeze penetrate his senses and swim in his veins.

As the two left, Cooper couldn't look at them. He held his eyes shut as if already sleeping. It would be hours before actual sleep arrived. Cooper tossed and turned throughout the night, fighting the shuteye that would end in stillness. He blinked awake and sat up to look at his clock over the bed. It was 12:28am. He laid back down to face his window, breathing in the outdoor evening air. Eventually, tears and exhaustion heavied first his eyes and then the rest of his body and Cooper nodded into the damning slumber.

Chapter 19

Catching the Tear

It seemed that only minutes had passed in the dreamless sleep of night. Although he was sure that they had just shut, Cooper's eyes snapped open quickly to the sound of a ringing telephone down the hall. In addition to the ringing, Cooper felt a warm tickle in the ear that was not against his pillow.

He didn't move.

He lay numb and still while staring at the window. He saw in the soft, orange light of early dawn, a very dim, weak firefly making a slow and tipsy flight out of his open bedroom window. Cooper's throat grew a suffocating lump; his mouth tasted salty and he felt the hot moisture welling up in his blurry, burning eyes but not falling. He pursed his lips tightly and swallowed hard while the phone continued to ring on.

"Hello?" his mom answered.

"April, it's your sister," Cooper heard his Aunt May exclaim excitedly.

"Hey, sis! Meant to call last night. Cooper got in just fine. Sorry I have you on speaker phone, I couldn't find the handset," Cooper's mom replied.

"It's okay. Derek and Cooper can hear this. It's great news. Just happened! You'll never believe it! I've just told Harry and I still find it difficult to imagine—so I just had to say it out loud again!"

Cooper listened stoically to the conversation. Listening would be something he'd have to get used to once again. He steadied his breathing.

"What?" asked Derek who must have just joined April.

"It's two miracles in one year. It's amazing!"

"Well, what is it?" questioned Cooper's mom.

"It's that boy; Danny Mills. He's the boy Cooper just visited."

"Yes?" prodded Derek.

"He woke up this morning and—" Aunt May broke off, choking back emotion.

"Are you okay?" April asked in concern.

"I'm great," Aunt May cried openly now. "I'm great. It's just that. Well—" Cooper knew what she would say before she finished saying it.

"-so is Danny," the words were tight with emotion. "He's great, too. He can walk, April. Danny Mills can walk. He woke up the same way our Coop did, April. His dad just called me and he's going to be fine. They never even found out what happened. So, there're going to be some tests. But, I just know it's okay. It has to be. I feel it. He couldn't move and now he can. I can't believe it."

Cooper tried to block out the rest of the conversation. His head ached deeply.

He blinked his eyes shut while his lips began to tremble and the tears that had formed in the bottom of his eyes squeezed out and began seeping out of his closed lids, streaming down to be absorbed by his pillow. The crawling wetness tickled as tears from his other eye made their way over the bridge of his nose while he lay on his side; the tear ran across his face and down the length of the cheekbone on the other side. As the itch grew in intensity, instinctively in that moment, Cooper reached up and wiped away the tear. He gasped at the sight of his own hand in front of his face.

"I . . ." he said to himself.

Cooper sat bolt upright in his bed disbelievingly. He sniffled and brushed away the remaining tears on his face. Then he stood. Immediately, Cooper's legs fell out from under him like a wobbly stack of books. He clunked loudly and heavily to the floor.

"Coop?" April called. "Hey, May, I gotta go. We'll talk later. Congratulations. I'm so happy for everybody. Please pass on our best," she rushed the words out.

"Will do! B'bye!" Aunt May happily finished before the tone of the speaker phone's good bye.

April shuffled down the hallway with Derek right behind.

"Cooper, you okay?" asked Derek.

"Why are you on the floor?" his mom wondered.

"I don't know," said Cooper, truthfully. "I fell. My legs don't feel right."

Chapter 20

Cooper Ridge, Ordinary Kid

Two weeks later, Cooper, his mom and Derek sat opposite the same doctor who was befuddled months ago with the miracle of Cooper Ridge, The Wonder Kid. They awaited the results of many tests and the answers to many questions.

"I don't know what to tell you," the doctor said. "There's nothing wrong with your son. In fact, it's quite the contrary. When you came to me in March, every test I performed seemed to tell me that your son shouldn't be moving at all. His nerves simply weren't carrying information the way they should. Yet, then, he was like an athlete. Now, he's . . . well . . . he's disabled, though certainly not the way he was. The difference now is that his nerves *are* working again."

"How did that change?" April asked.

"Perhaps they've repaired themselves because of all of their use. He's been an active boy and the human body is amazing. It's been known to heal itself with strong physical therapy and this summer has certainly served as that for him. All I know is that this at least makes some sense. That and it's the only theory I've got at this point," the doctor shrugged with a stumped expression.

"What does this mean? Will he ever be like he was, again?" said Derek.

"I see no reason he'd become paralyzed again," answered the doctor.

"No," Derek shook his head and looked to Cooper. "I mean . . . um . . . well, I don't want to sound ungrateful, but—"

"Oh. You mean will he be like he was in the summer. Anything's possible. If anybody has proven that, it's been Cooper. His legs work, Mr. and Mrs. Lowell. They're just weak. He'll need the walker until he's strong again. I'd have him practice walking without it for a little bit each day and I'd continue the same sorts of therapy you provided when he was in his chair. I'm sorry I don't have more answers for you. Do you have more questions for me?" he added.

"I just wish I understood why," April sighed with a reassuring squeeze around her son's shoulders.

"To that, I'll only repeat what I said in March. Medicine doesn't always have the answers. If I were in your shoes, I'd simply be grateful for the blessings I'd been given and I'd appreciate every moment I had," the doctor said while shaking his head as though he may loosen up some answers within it. Then he continued, resigned, "He has to learn to use his body. But, this is a natural process and one that we can all help him through."

"Do you want to ask anything?" Derek glanced kindly to Cooper.

"No. No, it's okay," Cooper said shaking his head. He half-smiled at Derek.

The three left very slowly as each step was one of agony for Cooper. He willed every muscle to move one leg at a time forward in an almost dragging motion. Cooper grimaced through the struggle, but never once complained about it.

Each day Cooper worked hard at becoming stronger. He earned every inch he moved forward, whether it was cheering in front of the stands at Nicholas' games, taking a neighborhood walk at night, or even moving across his own bedroom floor to turn his light switch on.

His overhead light and his bedside lamp were the only lights in his room, now—no longer were there fireflies. The dreams never came again after that summer; at least not the magical ones made of special memories. Cooper honestly didn't mind. For, each morning, he put his *own* arms around his mom. Each day, he used his *own* hand to shake that of his step dad. Each afternoon, he'd slap his best friend on the back or shoulder chummily when they sat on Nicholas' porch and while he felt the wetness of Beaches' tongue on his *own* cheek. Most importantly to Cooper, each quiet night, practicing

without his walker, using his *own* two legs—he took one more step
down the street.

He knew he'd make it to the end of the block one day and he knew
it was a destination that was earned and not stolen. While he worked,
just as they had when he was paralyzed and how they had when he
was an athlete—his mom and Derek loved him. Now, perhaps with a
better understanding than ever before thanks to a conversation with
the real Danny Mills, he loved them unconditionally and *selflessly* in
return

On his evening walks, Cooper often saw the fireflies flickering
in the distance, blinking beside the open windows of the children
in the neighborhood. His mouth would turn up sweetly as he was
overcome with quiet contentment for the secret of a fantasy world
that he would always keep. He was no longer Cooper Ridge, The
Wonder Kid and he never would be. He was; however, Cooper Ridge,
an ordinary kid.

A flood of warm satisfaction rushed through him when Cooper
realized that he was at peace with this title . . . perhaps even at *joy*.
As this thought of true happiness came over him, he saw a single
firefly—far brighter and far larger than any he had ever seen
before—appear seemingly out of nowhere in front of him. It floated
dreamily away from him and rose in a gentle drift up to the starry
sky above.